THE WILD NIGHT SKY

For Vicki, who inspired this collection

Crumps Barn Studio
No.2 The Waterloo, Cirencester GL7 2PZ
www.crumpsbarnstudio.co.uk

Cover design and illustrations by Lorna Gray

Printed in the UK by Severn, Gloucester on responsibly sourced paper

CARBON NEUTRAL

FSC www.fsc.org MIX Paper from responsible sources FSC® C022174

ISBN 978-1-915067-25-8

ZOEY BAKER
MICHAEL BARTLETT
AMARIS CHASE
HOLLY CRAWFORD
MYLES CUTLER
AMANDA JANE DAVIES
DAPHNE DENLEY
J. J. DROVER

THE WILD NIGHT SKY

Space stories and poetry, new worlds and earth

VICKI FLETCHER
BEVERLEY GORDON
HARRIET HITCHEN
ANDREW LAZENBY
REBECCA MCDOWALL
FRANK MCMAHON
ROSALIND NEWTON
JANE PHILLIPS
ANGELA REDDAWAY
ANNIE RIDER
MARGARET ROYALL

with illustrations by LORNA GRAY

Crumps Barn Studio

FOREWORD

Working with authors from all genres on a collection about space was always going to bring surprises.

Space is a common theme in Science Fiction, but the concept of living off-world is fast becoming a reality, at least for some, and possibly within our lifetimes. And writers have always had an uncanny ability to reflect the future.

When I was a child, I vividly remember reading *Tintin on the Moon.* As an adult, I revisited it and discovered that the book itself had been published in the early 50s. And yet the description of walking on the moon, the distance travelled, the physical forces upon the body at take-off and landing, even the concept of a rocket which might be reusable – all these things were already in the public psyche many years before Neil Armstrong spoke his famous words.

When it came to this book and the task of bringing together nineteen authors from across the UK for a collection of poetry and short stories, I knew I wanted to feel that same sense of scope for the future.

I also wanted to use their writing to take a closer look at our present experience of the night sky.

Humans have long had a complicated relationship with space. At times it is wondrous, sometimes it terrifies with the inconceivable scale of an expanding universe. Space is also a comforting spectacle, as a full moon rises over a treeline.

As the editor of this collection, I've had the opportunity to explore space anew. I've looked up at the stars from earth, and set foot on distant sands. I've discovered that there is mystery and bleakness, but hope can still be found in unexpected places.

Most of all, I've learned that our view of the wild night sky, wherever that may be, is always changing, always personal.

Lorna Brookes
Crumps Barn Studio

BLINKING LIGHTS

VICKI FLETCHER

Lights, blinking in the darkness. Your hands, unfamiliar – metal and silicone where flesh should be. You are voiceless – no scream emanates when you try, and staring into the reflective metal casing of one of the millions of servers that surround you tells you why – you have no throat, no breath, no mouth. Your body is not what it should be, that is the digital reconstruction you should be enjoying with the rest of humanity on this long journey through the stars to your new home. Your body, you are horrified to see, is one of the robotic caretakers tasked with maintaining the ship until you make it to your final destination.

Despair turns to anger. How could this have happened, you wonder – how could your mind have been uploaded into this thing? Anger turns to fear. How long is left of the journey – will you be conscious, unsleeping, for all of it? Fear turns to determination as you realise that if you can be uploaded to this body then you can be uploaded to the servers and rejoin humanity in digital paradise.

Weeks of trying quashes that idea and at last you realise the truth. You are trapped. You stare at your reflection and recognise nothing of yourself in the smooth metallic planes and expressionless blinking lights.

Determination mutates. You know the ship has 3D printers and synthesisers, should anything break and the caretakers need to repair something. They do not question your presence, just blink at you and accept you as one of their own. They allow you to begin your work unminded.

It is difficult work. You plan components based on the archives of humanity's many discoveries and understandings of science and anatomy. You begin to build, starting with a synthetic skeleton and moving on to artificial organs.

Occasionally you attempt to rejoin the digital collective but every time you are rebuffed. You don't know why you are rejected but you cannot stand the faceless visage that stares back at you from every direction. There are a lot of mirrors on this ship, you realise.

As you work you begin to talk to one of the robots you see most often. You name it Jay after the serial number stamped on its chest – JY-376. You don't look to see what is stamped on yours. Talking consists mostly of blinking at Jay and imagining responses. It's not the best conversation but it keeps you sane – you hope.

Years pass as you toil. Your project is shaping up at last, having proven to be a more difficult undertaking than you initially thought. Now it only needs a covering of synthetic skin and hair. You have had to learn everything from scratch as you worked, building prototypes and discarding countless failures – this one for being too short, that one for having something wrong about the shape of the face. You are certain it didn't resemble you, but as time marches on you grow less and less certain of what does.

Eventually the day comes when you realise you don't remember your name. The realisation sends shockwaves through your core and you blink in anguish at Jay.

"Do not worry," Jay blinks back. "You have a name like I do." He points to your chest and you read the serial code printed there – DN-014.

"You are DN," he blinks.

"DN," you respond. It sounds right. Content you return to your project. The hair will need replacing, you think. You are certain you weren't quite this blonde.

You spend more time talking with Jay and begin to realise how much you have in common. You both have the same sense of humour and enjoy the same stories stored in the archives – at least you think so. You can't actually get him to sit down and read them with you but you're sure he appreciates the cliffnotes.

Finally the day comes when you are confident the body is ready. It is perfect – flawless – and you plug the transfer cord in giddily. You open your new eyes and flex your fingers – not flesh but close – and feel at home. Your old body lies at your feet and you step over it, beaming.

You find Jay working amongst the server stacks and call out to him joyfully, marvelling at the sound of your voice echoing throughout the cold ship. He does not respond. You grab his sleek shoulder, starting to wear down with age, and greet him, introducing yourself and laughing. He blinks once and returns to his work. Your hands drop to your sides and your smile fades. You roam the ship, searching for any caretaker that will acknowledge you, but none do.

You find yourselves backed into a nook somewhere and allow artificial tears to fall from your eyes. Renewed despair floods you and you realise the only thing left to do is get yourself back into the databank with other humans. It didn't work before but surely you can find a workaround. You spend weeks trying and failing, the same message popping up with every attempt – *Invalid data.*

You punch the servers, cry and scream, and remain ignored by the caretakers. You become a ghost, walking among them. They blink to each other but their optics slide over you completely. You are invisible.

Finally you come to the realisation that arriving at your destination will be your salvation. You recall being told humanity was heading to a new planet some 300 lightyears away. You must be nearly there you think, based on how long you've been awake here. You begin your tireless search of the databanks for information on your destination and long journey. When you arrive humanity will reawaken and you won't be alone any more.

Your hopes turn to ash when you read the truth about your ship. There is no destination, you learn – there never was. The ship has been orbiting Earth the entire time, powered by the sun, as an ark. Humanity will never leave the confines of its digital existence, aside from you of course, and you will never rejoin them. You are alone.

The revelation nearly destroys you until you remember your old body – the metal one with DN-014 stencilled on its chest. Your only hope of company, of belonging, now lies with the caretakers. You race across the ship to the place you left your body. It is unmoved, silent. You jam the transfer cord in your neck and begin the countdown. When you come to it is with a great sense of relief. Your hands are metal and silicone, your mouth non-existent. You leap to your feet and go in search of your people, who you know will greet you with open arms and blinking lights.

SALTINGS

FRANK MCMAHON

Here nothing grows tall or large except the sky
stretched above this unflamboyant ground.

Vast, veined cortex, sea-washed, filled and drained,
negotiable land where wind and soil and water
work off each other in fluent stasis.

Salt tongues follow the pendulum of the moon
to bring their words twice-daily,
fill the creeks and channels; mercury-pulse,
whispers of assertion and withdrawal, gentle,
like the quiet telling of a story.

This is a place of modest colours: winter's
greylag geese among the sea-brite's orange tips,
prairie sagewort's silver-grey,
perennial curlew prospecting slick, mud banks
        for tidal gifts.
Restrained blue and pink of lavender and thrift.

This is a place for other lives,
where we can walk, wary of quags and brackish pools,
not with the redshank's careful tread
across voracious mud but on blue-baked clay.
We leave no footprint, merely a trace of our
passing through.

Boats are moored; optimistic plans
to find the open sea; others rust and rot
like discredited creeds and dogmas.

This is a place to come for silence
but welcome the wind and the oyster-catchers piping;
to open out as you walk
towards the sea, pause and return replete;
where tranquillity takes root and finds at least
a margin, perhaps a place more central,
a stab of joy in what you'd overlooked before,
a hope you could return and find again
a state of temporary grace.

This is a place where I lose and find myself.

IN THE FOOTSTEPS OF EARENDEL[1]

MARGARET ROYALL

The creature paused for the space of a star's breath,
then taking flight, like a speck of dust in
        cobweb tracery,
he will-o'-the-wisped away into the vast expanse of sky
up … up … away … and gone into the ether.

Yet his penumbra lingered, challenging me to follow,
though I knew not where or how … until
the sweet notes of a hypnotic song swanned across
the pools of my gathering tears and lifted me aloft
onto a stage, where costumed creatures alien to me
whirled and twirled across an ocean of golden spume,
chanting incantations in a language foreign to me.

---

1 Earendel has a dual meaning. Earendel appears in Tolkien's poem *The Voyage of Earendel the Evening Star.* It also refers to the star recently discovered in by the Hubble Telescope, the oldest and most distant star, which was similarly named.

As I trembled they pointed the way to a silken ladder,
which rose from invisible depths, blinding in its glory,
inviting me to clamber up and live the dream.
I leapt aboard, my ears assailed by the song
        of siren-folk,
ecstatic at my approach.

And then the scene faded, as though I were on
        the point of
fainting, ears buzzing, head spinning,
        colours fading to grey
and everything receding. My final thought was:
Where am I? Who am I? Where am I destined to go?
I was not the same me as before.

DEAREST EARTH

ZOEY BAKER

As work trips go, staying in a state-of-the-art home research facility in the middle of nowhere sounded like a dream come true.

Clara Hobbs was 25 years old and worked as a receptionist in her uncle's London headquarters. She never pretended to understand his work but she was a damn good people pleaser and kept up a convincing smile when faced with rich, pompous businesspeople – and that was good enough for him.

Stepping out of the helicopter she took in her surroundings. Green fields spread for miles, reaching a frost-tipped mountain range and large areas of woodland.

Clara was escorted a few feet away from the chopper by her chaperone.

"You need to walk straight for a mile." He pointed to a trail of pine trees.

Clara gave him a look that said you've got to be kidding me, but he simply shrugged, gave her a thumbs up and retreated to the helicopter.

It took an hour for Clara to reach the facility. It

was hidden amongst tall trees and sat on a cliff edge overlooking a ravine. The building itself could only be described as futuristic. The side overlooking the cliff was floor to ceiling glass. The rest of the building was windowless and light grey, blending into its cloudy surroundings. It was a long single storey facility; Clara imagined it could easily fit thirty rooms.

Clara reached what she assumed was the front door, the only indication being a screen to scan her ID card. There was beep before a section of wall slid open.

Clara followed the corridor round until she found herself in a square, homely living area. There was a stone fireplace, an L shaped sofa and bookcase against the wall. And to the left, up a couple of steps, was the kitchen with wall-to-wall windows overlooking the ravine, the mountains in the distance. A sense of calm washed over her.

Clara's only job for the next two weeks was to house-sit. To look after the place, keep it clean, and report any problems she came across whilst her uncle toured city to city from one billion-pound facility to another with his investors.

It should be a doddle, she thought.

Clara decided to explore, scanning her ID on pads next to every door she came across. Some flashed red, meaning access denied, but most of them turned green.

There was an indoor hot tub and spa room but it was the computer lab Clara found herself most comfortable in.

She sat in front of a computer and typed in her company login and password. The familiar Halcyon Labs logo spun in a circle as the desktop loaded.

Clara checked her emails but her uncle had assured her she wouldn't be disturbed unless it was an emergency. She was looking forward to no work for the next four weeks; she was about to log out when she saw something flashing in the top right corner of the desktop screen.

There was a popup envelope with the number 9 attached in bold where there hadn't been before.

Curious, Clara clicked on the icon. A series of white text appeared on a messaging system she was unfamiliar with.

E: Is anybody receiving this message?

E: I apologise for the inconvenience.

E: I seem to have gotten myself into an unfortunate situation.

E: I have found myself without navigation and would appreciate some assistance.

E: My name is Ezra.

E: I am currently in a ship approximately 200,000 kilometres from the surface of Earth.

E: My navigation system is broken.

E: I would very much be indebted to anybody who can help me.

E: I am most desperate.

Clara reread the messages, becoming concerned when she noticed the time stamps. The first had been sent ten hours ago but the last message had been sent a couple of minutes ago.

She knew exactly what she should do, and that is rattle off an emergency email to her uncle and his PA explaining what she'd found.

But something didn't feel right to Clara. And if somebody really did need help then the least she could do was try.

C: Hello Ezra. I might be able to help?

Ezra had been staring at his tablet for hours, praying that someone would receive his messages. When he wasn't looking at the screen he was watching the fuel gauge like a hawk. An hour ago the flashing light had gone from orange to red.

He ran a scarred hand through his messy brown hair. Ezra had been travelling in this ship for twenty one months. Nine months to Mars, three months collecting data and another nine back to Earth. It had been made clear to him that if anything happened he would be unable to ask for help because technically this mission didn't exist, funded privately and secretly by a man with too much money. Ezra once had confidence in his sponsor, but the ship was built with old tech; made to be untraceable, not reliable.

He had come so close. From his seat up in the sky Ezra could see the blues and whites of Earth. At least if I'm going to die, I couldn't ask for a better view, he thought grimly. But it wasn't in his nature to give up that easily.

As an act of caution Ezra had downloaded messaging software on his tablet a few weeks before he left for space, linking it to an IP address acquired when he'd visited his sponsor's home. In case something happened. And thank his lucky stars he did.

He would keep sending messages until his final breath, but there was a chance he would never step foot on Earth again.

The unfamiliar sound of a beep from his tablet startled him out of his thoughts. He held his breath.

C: Hello, I'm Clara. I might be able to help?

Ezra scoffed in disbelief. He looked away and rubbed his eyes, checking the tablet again to ensure he wasn't hallucinating.

It seemed somebody really had replied to his pleas. He eyed the fuel gauge. He couldn't waste any more time.

E: Good evening. I would be grateful for assistance. As per my previous messages you will know I am in a ship with no navigation system and cannot be guided back down to Earth without one.

His hands clenched and unclenched as he awaited a reply.

C: Is this real?

He would probably be a little cautious too if he found strange messages on his tablet from someone claiming to be from space. However, this person must be in the same computer room he had been shown around on his tour of his sponsor's home facility. They ought to know about him.

E: It is. My fuel is running low but I have enough to safely land if I begin my descent in less than twelve hours. Can you help me?

The skin on the inside of his cheek was bitten raw, but the pain reminded him that he was still alive. There was hope.

C: I'm not sure. What can I do from down here?

E: I need somewhere to safely land. It must be remote, with no chance of someone stumbling upon my plight.

C: Where were you going to land before your nav broke?

E: I have no idea. That information was stored in the Navigation System.

Ezra fiddled with the threads of his trousers, his uselessness frustrating him.

C: I will find somewhere, Ezra. Is there anything else I can do?

They were helping him. Ezra couldn't believe his luck.

E: I only ask that you keep me company.

Clara didn't actually know how to direct a ship to a safe landing place. Her research left her confused and more than a bit daunted by the prospect of trying to bring Ezra back to earth in one piece. Besides that pitfall, from what she could find there were no one-man missions to space, and no astronauts named 'Ezra'.

But if Ezra's fate rested in her hands, he couldn't deny Clara any nosey questions, could he?

C: How were you able to message me? Do you work for my uncle?

E: I believe your uncle is the sponsor of the mission I have been partaking in. He has, however, left me high and dry with no direct means of making contact. I took the details of the computer you are presently using to communicate with me when I last visited.

Clara supposed his story made sense. She knew her uncle's work was in the field of astronomy, even if she didn't understand it.

C: Are you saying he's tried to keep his involvement secret? Why would he do that?

E: This mission is confidential. Not even I know all the objectives behind it.

Clara felt unsure. What started off as curiosity was becoming overwhelming. If her uncle found out what would he do? Disown Clara? Fire her? Would any of that matter if she left a man stranded in space?

Clara's eyes darted from the maps on one computer screen to the messages on the other.

C: I'm going to get a drink. Be back in ten.

Clara entered the kitchen, switched on the coffee machine and sat at the island. Outside she could see a splattering of stars and wondered whether Ezra was looking down too.

She was overcome with the image of him floating in space for the rest of his days. When the fuel ran out would he spin out of control and crash land to Earth? Or would he be space junk for eternity? Clara was the only person who could decide his fate and that terrified her.

She had the sudden urge to want to go back to her boring, ordinary job that didn't involve life and death.

Clara filled a mug with fresh coffee, adding sweetener but leaving out the milk and walked back to the computer lab.

As she sat down she saw Ezra had sent another message.

E: What are you drinking?

C: Black coffee.

E: That's just how I like it.

C: I will make you the best damn coffee you've ever tasted when you get back.

She wondered if she would ever meet him.

E: I would be most thankful.

Clara turned to her other computer, searching Google Earth for an area large enough that a ship could land without anybody noticing. It was a lot harder than she thought.

E: Do you read?

Clara frowned. She was a bookworm when she was in school. But then she went to university and swapped out stories for reference books, and lost her love for fiction.

C: Not anymore. Life gets in the way, you know?

E: I understand. I brought a few books with me but I read them sooner than I anticipated.

C: I used to like the Narnia books. I wanted to be Lucy and be friends with Mr Tumnus. I spent hours in my mum's wardrobe waiting for the back to open up.

E: You are a lover of fantasy, how interesting. I've always preferred my literature on the morbid side. Lord of the Flies was a childhood favourite.

Clara snorted. So he was book smart. And funny – because there was definitely something deliberate about his choice of book, given their current situation. She liked the guy. She really hoped she could save him.

Ezra was happy. For nearly two years he had been on his own with no human contact and now he had someone to talk to.

C: Can I ask a question?

E: I am in no position to deny you anything.

C: Is there anybody I can contact? To let them know what's happened?

His smile turned forlorn as he thought of parents long buried and siblings he'd lost contact with long before he signed up for this mission.

E: There is no need for that.

Her kindness had gone beyond what he had asked of her.

E: But thank you for the thought. It is appreciated more than you can imagine.

Ezra cleared his throat and stood from the pilot's chair, stretching his legs. His back ached and his knees creaked as he awkwardly bent in the small space.

He was getting old. He had been a traveller all his life though he was more used to mountainous terrains than space. But the years of pushing his body to the limits had taken its toll.

Scars pulled taut in the wrong places, joints clicked when they shouldn't. He had planned to live a quiet retirement with the money earned from this mission. It would have been enough to see him into old age.

All he craved now was peace.

There was an island not far from New Zealand that was secluded enough that no one would notice the sudden appearance of a space capsule, but not too barren that there were no transport links to get Ezra back to civilisation.

C: It will be a few hours walk to a small village on the other side of the hills. Then you will need to take a 32 hour boat ride to the mainland.

E: That sounds delightful.

C: Is that sarcasm?

E: I have been in this ship for nearly two years. Why would you think a sudden long walk would be an issue?

C: This isn't funny. You won't be able to cope with 1G. I ought to send someone.

E: Clara, I have the luxury of artificial gravity. Courtesy of your uncle, I presume.

C: You could have mentioned that sooner.

Clara found the coordinates and Ezra helped with where he was in relation to Earth. Before they knew it Ezra was being guided back home.

C: You should wrap up warm when you arrive, it's cold in the southern hemisphere.

E: Will it be raining? I would give anything to feel rain on my skin.

C: Possibly. Are you sure I shouldn't try contacting someone who knows what they're doing?

E: I'm sure. You are doing a wonderful job. I can do most of the work from here, you just need to keep me company.

Clara sighed in relief. She opened up an internet tab and searched for a local news site in New Zealand. She'd keep it open over the next few days on the off-chance Ezra's landing made a buzz.

C: What else are you looking forward to?

E: Children's laughter. Dog fur. Warm sand between my toes.

Clara felt hopeless. Her job was done and all she could do was wait for Ezra to say everything had gone smoothly.

Over the course of the evening, in between toilet and coffee breaks, Clara and Ezra talked about everything and nothing.

E: As I make my final descent, I would like to convey my appreciation once more. I would be nothing but space junk if it wasn't for you.

E: Even if this is not successful, I am glad to have had a friend one last time.

Clara swallowed the lump in her throat. In a selfish way she was glad he found her too. In such a small amount of time Clara had grown attached to Ezra. She looked forward to his messages so much she hadn't been able to leave the computer lab for more than a few minutes at a time, not wanting to be separated any more than they already were.

C: I'm glad you found me.

Clara wanted to be honest.

Her fingers tapped rhythmically against the edge of the desk as she waited for a reply.

C: I mean it's been nice to talk to you. And I'm glad I could help.

Her heart was hammering. Had something gone wrong? Or was he simply too busy now he was close to entering Earth's atmosphere?

Clara refreshed the news page but nothing had changed. Of course it hadn't.

C: Ezra?

Her message was left unanswered.

SPACE SOUNDS

DAPHNE DENLEY

No morning calls of birds or other life scuffling about
I imagine mostly silence, maybe whistling,
    whizzing sounds

Distant bangs, as rocks collide, that float to
    randomly crash
Surrounding echoes, deep rumbling, crack of lights
    like fireworks flash

Noises fill the darkness, so mysterious this place
One can only dream of how things sound,
    way up in outer space

MOONSTRUCK
A MEMOIR

ROSALIND NEWTON

I would often sit by my bedroom window and gaze at the moon gleaming in the sky like a golden orb. I was a solitary child and would ask my parents "Is there really a man in the moon?" I never dreamt that one day I would meet a man who had walked on it.

My first flight was aged three in 1949. Not many people flew in an aeroplane for holidays back then. I remember being given a barley sugar to suck to stop my ears popping during take-off but it did not detract from the strange experience of the frighteningly steep ascent. Being strapped in a tight seat belt did not help me and I recall being relieved when my mother, who disliked air travel, released it. I also recall my father, who adored flying, talking to the air stewardess and afterwards I was given permission to visit the cockpit with my father to meet the Captain. I was fascinated by all the dials and instruments. It was very special to meet the man who had taken us up into the clouds.

Afterwards I felt much safer and coped well with the descent into Jersey airport. After many more flights as a child I became very interested when Sputnik 1, the size of a beach ball, was launched into space by the Soviets in 1959 and learned it was the first man-made satellite to provide valuable information for scientists about the upper atmosphere. I even taught my budgerigar to say "Hello Sputnik!" and this rendition became rather tiresome for my parents!

Sputnik's launch by the USSR had galvanised the Americans and the space race began. A new organisation was formed called the National Aeronautics and Space Administration (NASA). A variety of animals were put into space by both countries and I didn't like hearing about their deaths.

I was relieved when the Soviets launched Vostok 1 with a human cosmonaut, Yuri Gagarin, on board. The flight lasted about an hour and a half after one successful orbit and he returned safely to earth. The space race intensified.

Just three weeks later in May 1961 I was thrilled to watch the televised launch into space by an American astronaut, Alan Shepard, for a sub-orbital flight on Freedom 7 to test how a human could withstand the high forces of gravity and atmospheric re-entry to earth 230 thousand feet below. The flight lasted fifteen minutes, this was a dangerous exercise. Shepard safely splashed down in the Atlantic. Just three days later he was awarded the Congressional Medal by President Kennedy who was very committed to the US sending a man to the moon by the end of the decade. Sadly JFK's untimely death meant he did not see this goal achieved.

There were many space flights afterwards including one by Valentina Tereshkova, the first Soviet woman cosmonaut to fly solo in 1963. In July 1969 I was thrilled to watch the televised launch of Apollo 11 when Commander Neil Armstrong successfully reached the moon, and I recall hearing Armstrong's words as he walked on the lunar surface: *One Small Step for Man – One Giant Leap for Mankind.*

My dream had been realised; there was a man on the moon! More missions followed and on January 31st 1971 Apollo 14 was launched with Alan Shepard, Edgar Mitchell and Stuart Roosa on board. Alan Shepard had been grounded for some time because of an inner ear problem which required surgery. However, this American astronaut had a big surprise in store, hiding a specially adapted golf club plus two golf balls within his apparatus in order to play golf on the moon! The mission lasted until 9 February when the intrepid crew successfully splashed down in the Pacific Ocean from their module.

In 1988 I became Administrator of the first public Science Festival in Edinburgh and it was suggested that the perfect person to open it would be Alan Shepard. To my delight he accepted and gave an excellent talk to an excited audience about his two space journeys. Unfortunately the Director had to leave the event unexpectedly which left me in sole charge of a luncheon for our honoured guest to which the Lord Provost and the Festival's many sponsors had been invited. I had organised a special cake with a large iced rocket on the top. During the main course I was approached by the chef who whispered that the rocket was in danger of sinking into the cake.

After some quick thinking I arranged to have the cake brought in before the pudding so it could be cut first by Alan Shepard. Problem solved and all seemed well. I was thus unprepared to receive a telephone call the next morning from Alan Shepard asking me to come to his hotel to meet him as he needed to discuss an issue.

I was panic-stricken as I feared the "Icy Commander" – as he was sometimes known – must have been displeased with the event, but, on the contrary, I was greeted by a grinning Shepard, who, over coffee, requested that extra photos of the cake be sent to him, commenting that it was the most phallic-shaped iced rocket on a cake he had ever seen! Much relieved I returned to the office with a smile on my face.

Some time later I became Director of the High Blood Pressure Foundation, a medical research charity based in Edinburgh, and went hot air ballooning wearing an electronic blood pressure monitoring device to see if the flight had affected mine. Alan Shepard heard about my exploit, sending a very witty letter as we had stayed in touch.

I knew that astronauts had tested new medical equipment during missions so I invited him to give another talk in aid of the charity. Admiral Shepard accepted my invitation and returned in September 1996. He described his excitement at collecting lunar rocks that no one had touched for four billion years, looking at Planet Earth with the sun shining on its surface and oceans and ice caps a quarter of a million miles away, feeling that he could hold the earth in the palm of his hand.

Whilst choosing the menu for the event I decided there should be no cake!

I did not realise that Rear-Admiral Alan Shepard, brave naval aviator, test pilot, and astronaut, was being treated for leukaemia at the time, dying in 1998. I remain proud to have known him.

VILLANELLE FOR THE FIRST MEN ON THE MOON

MARGARET ROYALL

Those first three men who landed on the moon
Were surely hoping they would all survive
Their families prayed they'd fly home safely soon.

They showed great calm and strength, a massive boon
Though privately they all feared for their lives
Those first three men who landed on the moon.

They listened to the radio's poignant tunes
Reminding them of children, home and wives
Their families hoped they'd fly home very soon.

Sometimes to lift their mood they'd play the goon
With playful space-manoeuvres, swerves and dives,
Those first three men who landed on the moon.

They gathered moon rocks lunar winds had strewn
Ate food from tubes, no use for forks or knives
Their families hoped they'd fly home very soon.

Job done they launched their craft into the gloom
Like honey bees that buzzed back to the hive.
Their families glad they'd flown back very soon …
Those first three men who landed on the moon.

ONE DAY

DAPHNE DENLEY

Washing up bottle clenched in hand
"Rocket commander, coming into land"

Through the stratosphere it soared,
dodging household obstacles galore

"Firing boosters, up and away"
Through atmosphere, crossed into space

A hero's welcome, as mummy claps
"Been to the moon, and now I'm back"

Mission only for the brave,
commander Ben, history has made

"Today the moon, tomorrow it's Mars"
Imagination, beyond the stars

In bed his favourite planetary mobile,
spins above, he looks in wonder

And dreams of travelling up in space,
an astronaut will be one day

AN UNEXPECTED EVENT AT THE SPACE CENTRE

MARGARET ROYALL

'Come on, it'll be fun! Don't be such a spoilsport.' Carol was buoyed up by her spur-of-the-moment plan to escape the dreich November weather by spending a day at the local Space Centre with her husband Phil. As someone with a degree in astrophysics she was a keen follower of all things outer space and this was somewhere she'd always wanted to visit.

Phil, however, was less enthusiastic, being a creative soul who liked to spend his leisure time writing short stories, painting watercolours and taking photographs.

'I think it's more a children's thing,' he said, 'not really for adults, probably quite boring.'

'How do you know if you've never been? You really are a stick-in-the-mud. And anyway, I've bought tickets online and we're going – anything better than staring at this endless downpour.'

Phil could see her mind was made up and decided for once to stop complaining and go along with her plan.

'Ok, you win. Jump in the car and I'll drive us there,' he said.

From the outside he thought the building looked uninviting, though he had to admit that the 42 metre high semi-transparent rocket tower was quite something. It was visible from all approach routes and, once through the museum doors, he had to admit to himself that the whole complex did look more interesting than he had dared to hope (though pride prevented him from actually saying so).

'Where shall we start?' said Carol, unfolding the guide to the centre. 'I want to see absolutely everything, but my first choice would be the show in the Patrick Moore planetarium. Shall we go there?'

Phil wasn't fussed. 'Whatever you want,' he said and stomped along behind her up the escalator into the planetarium theatre. There were several thrilling shows to see with such captivating titles as We are Stars, We are Aliens, We are Astronomers and most amazing of all The Night Sky. They craned their necks looking up at the breath-taking light show projected on the dome above them.

Carol was riveted throughout, gasping in wonder and tapping her husband's arm whenever she wanted to draw his attention to something truly amazing. Phil grunted his approval at regular intervals. He actually found the shows an eye-opener but was too stubborn to show his enthusiasm. He thought that the Rocket Tower might be somewhere that would fire up his creative juices and maybe provide material for a short story, so once the planetarium shows were finished he suggested they go there next. The guide stated that the iconic Rocket Tower housed the centre's most thrilling artefacts: the Blue Streak and Thor Able rockets, as well as the Gagarin Experience, Apollo Lunar Lander and real Moon Rock. Now that sounded more like it. Phil dared to feel excited.

Indeed, the exhibits proved fascinating and while Carol rushed back and forth exclaiming each time she encountered ones that provided her with new information, Phil decided to do some close up photography in the hope of being able to illustrate the short story now forming in his head.

He concentrated so hard on achieving the right perspective and trying out different techniques that he got totally carried away by the new project. Suddenly he felt exhausted and needed to sit down. By this point his wife had grown tired of waiting for him to finish and had informed him in no uncertain terms that she'd had enough and was off to the café to grab a coffee and slice of cake.

'Remember to keep your phone switched on, please. I'll text you when I'm finished.'

'Ok, go ahead, I'll join you shortly,' Phil had said, 'I just need to get the angle right on this Gagarin shot. My mobile will be on anyway, I'm going to dictate notes to my voice memo.

He took a few more shots and once satisfied with the resulting photos he looked round for somewhere to sit, but there were no seats provided. However, he remembered noticing a door in the room adjacent marked *Rest Room – Staff Only*. Ignoring this he tried the handle and the door opened into a small room with comfy sofas and a coffee table. It was empty. Ah, just the ticket, surely no one would mind? he thought, slumping down on a well-used settee. It was then he noticed a stout chest in the corner marked *Fancy Dress*. The lid was open and a pile of clothes was spilling out. On top was an astronaut costume, probably intended for a lanky teenager. Still a child at heart, Phil simply couldn't resist trying it on and taking a quick selfie, admiring himself in what he took to be a strange little mirror set into the wall. He then sat back down, closed his eyes and started imagining the opening sequence to his next story. As new ideas formed in his mind he recorded voice notes on his iPhone. Just a quick ten minutes, then he'd join his wife in the cafe, he told himself.

Suddenly he was startled by an ear-splitting whoosh, accompanied by the weird sensation that he was hurtling upwards into space. He tried to grab hold of the bench but it had disappeared and he found himself floating weightlessly around inside a space capsule. The strange thing was he didn't feel at all scared … just totally elated. The weightlessness was utterly thrilling.

'Wow, look at me, I can't believe I'm flying through space!' His jubilant voice boomed from inside the space helmet.

He tried out various manoeuvres that he'd seen in footage of space flights on TV. Could he turn somersaults? Wow, yes, he could, though rather clumsily, as he ended up banging his helmet against the wall and being catapulted into the control desk with its hundreds of levers, buttons and flashing lights. Now this was fun, he thought to himself, much better than a dreary afternoon at home looking out at the rain. He pondered where he might be heading. The moon? Mars? He imagined himself about to make history, imagined the newspaper headlines:

Local Author Creates History on Space Voyage

As he floated past a large porthole window he looked out and saw far below him the curvature of the earth, oceans, landmasses, wonders beyond his wildest dreams. Then glancing upwards into the velvet blackness of space he marvelled at the millions of twinkling stars, so dazzling it took his breath away. He felt he could stay here forever, maybe even land on the moon, be a reincarnation of Neil Armstrong? Anything seemed possible.

What suddenly occurred to him as odd though, was that he appeared to be alone on board. Shouldn't there be other crew members? Where on earth where they? Surely he was not expected to man this craft single-handedly?

At that very moment an alarm began to sound and lights began flashing on the control panel. The buzzing grew louder, more insistent and now more red lights started flashing. His exhilaration switched instantly to panic. What was he supposed to do?

'Help, help, is there anyone here? Somebody help me please!'

His head began to spin as blood drained from it and he feared he might black out completely. He clutched the control desk, willed himself to stay alert, desperately casting his eyes about, hoping to see another crew member emerge from a recess. The noise was deafening and now every single light was permanently on and the sign DANGER illuminated on the wall.

'SOS, SOS, we're going to crash. I'm going to die,' he yelled at the top of his voice.

Just as he found himself at the point of no return his panic was abruptly interrupted by a familiar voice, speaking sternly to him. Then someone was shaking him roughly by the shoulders in an irritated manner,

'Wake up, Phil, come on now, it's time to go home, the museum is closing,' said the voice.

Slowly Phil forced his eyes open. It took him a few seconds to gather his wits and realise that he was still in the hub's staff room dressed as an astronaut, alive and unharmed. The relief he felt at that moment was akin to euphoria. Yet he was not out of the woods, as beside him, with a face like thunder, stood his wife, demanding an explanation.

'What on earth are you doing still here after all this time dressed in that ridiculous costume?' she said. 'You shouldn't even be in here, it's private. There are cameras monitoring the place, you know. Heaven knows what was in your mind, you were screaming out in terror for help. When you didn't join me in the café I tried repeatedly to get hold of you, but you didn't answer your phone. I was worried sick, but thankfully the curator eventually found you here. He's very annoyed. Everyone has gone and he needs to lock up. Pull yourself together. We need to get going!'

Phil was more than a little embarrassed and apologised lamely. He realised he had caused great anxiety and had made a real fool of himself. Sheepishly he followed his wife out to the car and sat in sulky silence as she drove them back home. He resented her treating him like a naughty child and her failure to understand and appreciate his creative impulses. He resolved to get his own back by playing a prank on her. Yes, that was what she deserved. A brilliant idea came to him.

On arrival home he tried to tell her what had happened to him in the rocket, describing the wonders he'd seen through the spacecraft windows and then the horror situation which unfolded. She indulged his fantasy but her laughter was clearly more derisory than sympathetic and he could tell she was simply indulging him. His resentment grew.

After supper they sat down in the lounge to watch TV and Phil checked his phone. He noted with surprise that the voice memo he'd recorded was much longer than he'd estimated and on plugging his earphones in and playing his notes back it became clear that he'd also recorded his excited commentary in the spacecraft and his cries of terror.

'So, my love, just listen to this,' he said to Carol. 'Here's undeniable proof that I actually did take off in a rocket today!' He steeled himself for her mocking response.

But just as he was about to pass her the phone a newsflash blitzed across the TV screen, stopping him in his tracks, making the blood drain once again from his cheeks.

Reports are just coming in that a spacecraft has burned up on re-entry. Sadly the lone crew member has perished. As yet the astronaut has not been named. Further details will follow.

VANISHING OF THE ISS

VICKI FLETCHER

The vanishing of the ISS five years ago became the greatest unsolved mystery of our time. There had been no indication anything was about to happen. Its personnel reported everything as normal right up until the moment it suddenly vanished from our sky.

NASA, naturally, went ballistic, as did every other space program on Earth. One moment the station was there, serenely orbiting the planet, and the next the computers were showing nothing. Engineers, scientists, management, interns – even the guy who worked the canteen – everyone was scrambling to figure out something, *anything*.

It must have had a foreign body collide with it, one desperate astrophysicist offered, but there was no debris, no shooting stars as chunks of the ISS fell to Earth. Press conferences were held, presidents and prime ministers all gave shades of the same speech: *unforeseen tragedy, our hearts go out to the families of the astronauts.* Eventually there was nothing more to be done, to be said.

Talks began on the idea of constructing another station – one contributed to by more countries than before – but public opinion was divided on the idea. After all, they argued, who was to say the same thing wouldn't happen again.

With time the world moved on. Remembrance days were held every year on the anniversary and the papers began reporting on other matters. The Mystery of the ISS, as it became known, was quickly relegated to conspiracy forums, each theory being put forward more ludicrous than the last. Armchair detectives pored over the event tirelessly, certain they would solve what NASA could not. Surprising no one, they didn't.

Then, five years to the day after the station vanished, the message came through. It was just five words but the effect they had roared through NASA, the media, the world. Headlines everywhere printed the message verbatim: *ISS incoming. All astronauts aboard.*

The world on tenterhooks, eyes cast upwards, humanity held its collective breath. There were celebrations and parties. Amateur and professional stargazers alike took to their telescopes, hoping to be the first to spot the station back in the sky. Scientists and talk show hosts began discussing the darker possibilities behind the message. It had been in English, sure, but who was to say it had come from friendlies.

SETI began beaming a reply in the direction the message had been sent from, but there was no immediate response. Then, a few weeks after the first message came a second. This time it was just one word: *Incoming.*

There were fewer parties this time. The populace had been bombarded with what ifs and many now considered the message warily. "Why don't they send more messages?" it was asked, but no satisfactory answer could be found. Meanwhile, militaries worldwide quietly prepared for the worst.

In the middle of June it happened. As abruptly as it had vanished from the sky five years prior, suddenly the ISS was back. There had been no incoming body, stated NASA, no indication the station was about to arrive. It just … appeared.

NASA immediately tried to make contact and after a few unsuccessful attempts they finally did, asking the ISS to check in the moment a connection was made. Several heart-stopping, static-filled moments later a man's voice filled the room: "All astronauts alive."

The room exploded with cheers and applause. Press conferences were held, the world celebrated. Shuttles were prepared for launch to bring the survivors home and find out exactly what had happened.

The shuttles docked without issue, reported their pilots once they had returned home and were in the process of being debriefed. Many cups of coffee and tea were pressed into their trembling hands as they told their stories.

"Everything seemed normal," one said in a hollow voice. "The airlock pressurised and we opened the door, thinking we were heroes. Thinking we were going to bring the vanished astronauts home. We …" Her voice cracked and she was unable to continue, merely shaking her head when pressed. Her state-appointed psychologist cut the interview, stating that shock such as this had to be dealt with gently.

"We left them up there," said another member of the rescue crew. "We couldn't bring them back to Earth – not like that. I don't know if that was the right thing to do but you have to understand, we couldn't even tell what they were at first. It was only when they opened one of their mouths and repeated their last message—"

"All astronauts alive?" inquired the interviewer.

"Yes. Then we knew. Whatever they'd become, we couldn't bring them home. You have to understand," he pleaded, eyes wide. "We wouldn't have been able to fit them on a shuttle. Not merged together like they were."

The Mystery of the ISS was never officially resolved. Plans to build another station were quietly shelved and the official government byline was that the messages were pre-recorded, that upon inspection the station was found to be empty. Not long afterwards an explosion did what many had speculated had happened to the ISS in the first place and the space station was destroyed. Reports of missiles being fired at it from the surface were quickly swept under the rug, becoming the talk of conspiracy theorists only. Another smaller memorial was held for the brave crew who had, as far as the world was aware, perished some time earlier.

Behind closed doors powerful people vowed never to send humanity into space again – just in case.

THE CRAB NEBULA

ANNIE RIDER

Far above us
Beyond the blue, the black
The white and the grey
Miracles lie
Beyond our eye.
Visions beyond imaginations
A vast universe
Enriched with perpetual
Capricious formations.
Parting gifts from
Exploding stars
As they give birth to
New creations
The brilliant nebulas
And the supernovas.

One such miracle discovered
Many centuries ago
The first of its kind
The first to know
Was the Crab Nebula
Born of a large star
Which ignited in the sky.
Seen from afar
By eastern stargazers
Witness to the birth
Of this supernova remnant
Above our Earth.

In its heart
Beats the heart of the star
A dense and dancing pulsar
Growing by the day
Brighter, more powerful
Than our brilliant Sun's ray.

Eleven thousand light years away
Beyond our vision with naked eye
Too dim in the sky
So the need to magnify
To observe its majesty.
Placed between stars
Zeta and Betelgeuse
And the constellations
Orion and Taurus.

Then only seen
In the North between
Autumn and Spring
Summer in the South.
With telescopic vision
The visualization
Of this wonderous supernova
Relic of an unknown star.

Marvel at the beauty
Of its impressive majesty
Hidden deep in the universe
With a multitude of others
All of a beauty beyond us
Some known to us,
Some yet to know
To be discovered
Formed and revered.

FUTURE BEYOND

DAPHNE DENLEY

Lynn climbed earth's highest mountains,
    into cold skies above
As nothing left behind her and no one there she loved
Heaven might be closer, be reunited with those old
In bitter wind words whisper, from friends and
    family's souls?
Hiking further up and higher, the air gradually thins
Feet and toes lost feeling and head now in a spin
Is this the final moment, as thinks her time has come?
Looks to the sky to take her, letting go,
    hands held above
Frozen in the moment her body starts to rise
Earth below her feet slowly moves farther from sight
Barely able now to breathe, eyes heavy but must look
Vigorously heart is pumping, body's just not giving up
Suddenly the skies are black and earth seems
    miles away
Looking to the distant stars, is that the Milky Way?
Lynn's arms and legs turned grey and black,
    skin's fragmented dust

Finger nails are shining silver, polished to a buff
Disoriented and confused, realises, so amazed
Looks everywhere, can float around, she's actually up
in space
For a while, then flies at will, like super hero brave
Pieces caught of passing rocks, can crumble
them away
Suddenly she spies some land, a planet just like ours?
Tentatively glides forwards, through meteors and stars
Closer body pulled to drop, now sitting on some rocks
A purple river down below her reflection
first time clocked
Hair is golden like metallic threads and eyes are
piercing blue
Lips are white like lightning bolts, body cloaked
in fabrics new
Over the river, another being, Lynn is not alone
Alien only as unknown, but a similar looking clone
It flies towards, their eyes both fixed, speaks in its
mother tongue
Who would have known, but strange they hugged,
was destiny to come?
A new beginning on planet x, is that what
will become?
Our future written in the stars, as Alien Space Persons

A SPACE TO CALL ONE'S OWN

J. J. DROVER

Barney lay back in his deck chair watching the sunset, sipping contentedly from a glass of iced tea. No matter how many times he watched this, it was always with a sense of wonder as one by one the triple suns set serenely over the fizzing sea.

A warm breeze wafted across the beach bringing with it the citrusy smell of the flowers that grew amongst the rocks at this end of the island. It was the end of another beautiful day here on his new home planet.

As he sat and watched, he mused on the idea that for a great deal of human civilization, the transport of goods and passengers between various destinations had been the preoccupation and also the study of many peoples; traders, business, explorers, holiday makers, scientists and engineers alike. Increasing the speed whilst lowering the cost of travel and transport had been the goal, a holy grail or, Barney chuckled to himself, a destination in itself you might say. But this industrialised race to travel faster and save money was ultimately pointless. The one race they could never win was time. And time is money.

But a change came, and a solution (of sorts) was found, when it was realised that both the moderate distances that separated the terrestrial destinations and therefore the vast distance of intergalactic space could be bent, twisted and folded through the application of some fairly rudimentary particle acceleration technology and a small change of perspective. Through this new technology the scientists found they now had the ability to travel, almost instantly, anywhere in the available universe, and human civilization was no longer trapped on its restrictive and under-resourced home planet. The dream of travelling to distant stars had at last been realised.

It was whilst researching the movement of sub-quantum particles that the scientists realised how a certain action one location had the potential to happen in an almost infinite number of other locations at the same moment. And when two actions were made to happen at the same moment their respective locations were interchangeable. And so it was found that merely being in one place was the same as being in another.

The patent for this technology was hotly debated and disputed with many arguing that the esoteric philosophies and ideologies from many cultures, contemporary and historical, had already claimed this knowledge. The fundamental ideas that there is only 'here and now' and that we are all belonging to a universal oneness, were so ideologically ingrained that to attempt ownership of the idea was preposterous. But nonetheless, business being business, enterprise fought and won. The technology was patented and many rich people got richer.

During history lessons Barney remembered learning how throughout the long ages when humans were trapped on earth, everyone fought for their own little space. This regularly led to leaders forcing a population to fight to gain control over other people's space. But now the universe was accessible it was discovered that there was space enough for everyone. There were an infinite number of habitable planets within an infinite space, all now within reach thanks to this new form of travel.

The pioneers leapt at the chance of travelling the vast, indeed almost incalculably vast, distances to seek out those mythologised new civilisations and lifeforms that had been long speculated on. The old pioneering call to 'go west my son!' was taken up once again as a rallying cry, though direction really had little to do with it anymore. And when looked at from the perspective that made such travel possible, nobody really went anywhere at all, as all the places anyone went were intrinsically connected to the departure lounge (as it became known) of Universal Exports Inc., the original patent holder of the technology used to transport everyone everywhere.

This monopoly on universal travel was short-lived though with the release of a set of fairly simple DIY plans that bypassed the complicated technology held by Universal Exports Inc. A group of free minded young scientists saw the obvious loophole in the technology and made it freely available to the public before any of the multinational companies could act. The vastness of the universe should be free from the corporate tyranny they declared. And so began a new era of human civilization.

Indeed, it was discovered that space was so vast, it contained planets enough that everyone could have one of their own, and for a while it seemed that was exactly what everyone wanted. Barney remembered the novelty factor of owning an entire planet. Earth had become not only overcrowded but polluted, and the opportunity to escape all this was now available.

Barney's family, along with nearly the entire population of the planet, had done just that; packed up and left the old ways behind to live in a new kind of Eden world of their choice. Many families took the concept of planetary ownership to the point of each family member inhabiting their own solitary world. The idea was that each planet became a notional room within the old-fashioned idea of a family home. The ideas about size and distance had been irrevocably altered. Travel between these planet rooms was now as simple as walking through a door. Albeit with a bit of a leap into intergalactic nothingness between rooms. Most people had no idea how this technology worked, they just knew how to operate the machines that they had made or purchased. This though, was the case for nearly all the technology used throughout history, so little changed and nobody really worried about it.

For a while humanity scattered themselves to the furthest reaches of the universe and had little or no contact with anyone else. This was an obvious reaction to the terrible times of the great Climate Catastrophe of the twentieth century. People needed to breathe and feel a bit of space around them. But this was a temporary state and soon it became apparent that a curious outcome of having so much space was that people began to cluster with many deciding to leave their isolation to form small communities on single planets. Often, this included invoking the village gods of old.

Barney spent a number of years living in isolation and felt better for it. He had always enjoyed solitude, even as a child, and those years had been spent in quiet contemplation like the Zen masters Barney had read about.

But now Barney felt that he had found his home here on this planet, within this little community. He had found friends and family. It was true what they said, he mused, just the idea of having space was enough for most, and what they actually wanted was to enjoy all that space in the company of others.

ESCAPE

DAPHNE DENLEY

Empty mind, empty the mind, I chant this to myself
As life's become so overwhelming, damaging
    my health
Eyes screwed shut, arms hugged round sides,
    muscles tensed so tight
Droning noises getting in, shake head to
    block them out
I had a dream was in the trees, deep into forest life
And only sounds of birds that tweet, by day and
    hoot by night
Sometimes in dreams on empty beach, asleep on
    sun drenched sands
Only woken by rising tides, swishing over toes
    or hands
Hiding in the wardrobe or running from my day
It's really not an option, doesn't make it go away
And as much as I now struggle, and do put on
    this brave face
I really must remember, that in dreams
    I find some space

NEBULA

REBECCA MCDOWALL

The dust from the death of another ancient star drifted in a stupor across the galaxy of the Huntress. Lazily following the path that all dust found itself drawn to in the wake of a star's death. There never seemed any urgency to it, they were allowed to follow along in a peaceful slumber. Drifting without care. Each glowing ember still so exhausted from its recent demise that it didn't really pay attention to the path it was being summoned to, or to the lullaby that played sweetly across the vast expanse, soothing them all like a mother's kiss. Each ember's glow slowly dimmed as its fever broke.

Every star fears its death. It hadn't always been that way, but fear spreads far quicker than fire. The black hole that will swallow it in all its destructive glory. Leaving behind only further desolation for any that dare to approach the monstrosity. Many thousands of centuries ago the stars had reached an agreement that had withstood the test of time. Each star had promised that when it was sure that it was reaching the end of its natural cycle it would let off warning flares for those who were inside of its solar system and neighbouring impact zones. Allowing them to move as far away as they could from the dying star before the black hole made its appearance. The treaty provided the dying star some solace that they wouldn't be responsible for bringing as many other stars with them into the beyond. Instead, they would shine on.

The mother had tried countless times to teach her children that they were wrong to fear death this way. Before she allowed her children to take up their places shining their beautiful souls across the vast darkness of space, bringing life wherever their rays touched, she spoke to each one of them about the beauty of death. The mother painted beautiful tales of how the welcoming embrace of death would finally extinguish the fury of the fever flame, its cool embrace bringing with it a certain peace that they would never have felt before. How they would tumble with joy in their hearts as they found themselves finally unravelling within the black hole's gentle care. No longer forced to stay for millennia stuck in a circular form but now newly demised and finally for the first time since their birth they found themself free and surround by their billions upon billions of brothers and sisters.

Their eternal mother had filled the sky with shooting stars demonstrating to her newborn children the peaceful path they would float down when their star finally ceased. The journey that after a few more thousand ages would reunite her children with their mother. When finally at their journey's end, and in the form that they had been born into this world in, they would all vibrate in harmony, forming a new peaceful universe.

But despite almost fourteen billion years of telling her children this truth about the peaceful demise that awaited them at the end, it was not enough. Nebula the eternal mother had had reached the end of her patience. She had hoped that by telling them the truth from the moment they were dust, to have left them prepared and filled with understanding before sending them out into the expanse, that this knowledge would have kept them from the fear that dulled their flames. A fear that prevented them from bringing further life to the universe. Honesty had not been enough. She wasn't sure when it first began. The first few billion years seemed to go just as she had hoped. But lately, fear rampaged through her children. Whispers spread amongst the stars of the peril that waited for them beyond the horizon of the black holes. With each whisper, the fears grew, and the light of the stars dimmed further, until their beauty was no longer the beacon that they had once been renowned for.

Nebula had spent the last three hundred thousand years searching for a way to help her children but nothing in the scrolls seemed to offer her the answer that she so desperately longed for. Instead, they offered her a chance to reset. It would plunge the universe into the darkness of eternal night and wipe her children from existence for now. But she would be able to rebirth them, tackle whispers head-on, stop the poisonous fear from spreading and create a second chance to be with them throughout the swallowing. To show them how to burn brighter than they ever thought possible, to breathe life into new planets.

The mother gazed at the lights that twinkled across the great expanse in wonder, at everything she had worked so hard to create. With a single tear of regret Nebula plunged the universe into darkness.

It went silent as every planet froze over. Eternity on pause.

HEAT DEATH

FRANK MCMAHON

Meeting by chance, from other orbits,
the air crackled, gravity pulled
in an opposite direction. Random chance
became negotiated patterns and hyperactive starbursts,
the prospect of infinity naive but fully charged.

Shared haloes of unfettered speech,
sharp-elbowed fights, erotic reparation
on deserted beaches, in midnight bars,
fuelling their incandescent core.

Time warped and stretched, impossible
to evade the wear and drain of entropy.
Their stars drew apart; each trailed
a smirr of background radiation
the other ceased to track.

PILOT EPISODE

HARRIET HITCHEN

This, thought Captain Elizabeth Finch, was a mistake.

Crouching in the dark behind a small heap of containers, she only had a partially obscured view of the landing bay. A group of guards was moving from the command station, an untidy huddle hefting weapons – both conventional guns and sonic. The sort that left no mark but took a person apart from the inside.

Her armour gave some protection. But they'd stripped all that from the man they were pushing along in their midst. To the point that he looked obscenely bare – like he was naked.

They'd left him in his trousers and shirt, so he wasn't actually undressed, but it was obscurely shocking. Perhaps it was because they'd taken his shoes.

Finch kept him in her sights. He was Jack Wall – her second in command and he wasn't supposed to be here. The night sky was black like the edge of the universe. It was the sort of darkness that seeped into your bones. There were guards on the twin lookout platforms and they weren't happy. They were shouting questions at each other and gesticulating at the shuttle which lay in a sea of freight and abandoned forklift trucks. It was absurd that of all the exports from earth, the forklift was the tool that had made it this far.

Jack looked as if the past seven hours had been rough. They were shoving him along towards the shuttle. If they got him on board that was it. He was gone.

Against these numbers, with the resources these people had, the odds weren't good.

She lobbed the flare grenade at the furthest stack of provisions.

She ducked her head into the crook of her arm. Counted three seconds then opened her eyes. The rifle was ready in her hands. Sighted disoriented guards. Two fell. A third fumbled blind with his weapon. Dropped it. Four. Five.

Pressed the remote in her sleeve. Nothing happened. Cursed. Fired two shots at the nearest of the guard platforms. Flung another flare grenade. Shielded for a count of three and then she was up and running, keeping low until she reached the man who was crouching with his head between his knees and shackled wrists over his head.

"Jack."

He lifted his head. The blindness from the first flash was fading and he'd had the good sense to shield his eyes from the second.

They caught their breath behind a stack of crates. Darkness was their friend. Floodlights were coming on with a pop, one by one along the boundary wall.

"Where's the crew?"

"Creating a diversion."

Three minutes behind time, but blessedly on cue, there was a distant boom. Red flared briefly. The sky was lower than she'd thought. Heavy with clouds. Then a roar of engines as the ship – *her* beloved ship – burst free of its moorings and ground its way overhead.

"What about the cargo?"

"What did I just say? Diversion."

A sideways glance caught the way his mouth had tightened into a line. "Stars above, Bess—"

She silenced his concern with a scowl. The ramifications for dropping the job were bad. And yes, she'd entrusted control of the ship to the engineer Marco. Yes, that meant she'd undertaken this action on her own, at her own risk. No, she didn't remotely trust that Marco wouldn't abandon her. *Them.* It was a beautiful ship.

There was always a cost when things went wrong. And this jaunt had gone badly wrong.

She dug out the bootlegged key to remove his handcuffs. Handed him the pistol from her holster.

"Thanks." He propped his back against the stack of crates while he checked the cylinders in the gun. He clicked the chamber shut. "Now what?"

"Rendezvous."

And hope against hope that Marco is there. She didn't add that part. She didn't need to. Jack knew the condition of her small and misfit crew as well as she did.

Probably better. As her deputy he was partially immune to the isolation that came with her rank.

Keeping low, always keeping low, she led a cautious route through the stacks of provisions. The guards were busy panicking over the fire in the distance – the valuable cargo they ought to have been protecting rather than ogling the extradition of a man like it was an entertainment show.

There would, however, always be one guard with more brains than the rest. Finch knew this, she just didn't know whether they would be better at hiding than she and Jack were.

There.

She didn't need to point. Padding soft-footed behind her, Jack eased into a crouch. Briefly lifted his eyebrows as a question.

There was a team of five guards. They were stalking a parallel course. Weapons at the ready. Sonic weapons.

Jack used the crook of his arm to steady his aim. Ready.

Silently, Finch eased the riffle into position. Sighted. Stilled her racing heart. Fired.

Fired again when she missed.

In fairness, she was aiming at the metal cable keeping a signal mast in position. Her second shot finished what the first shot had only clipped. The cable whipped like a live wire.

Five guards scattered when the mast fell. Scattered again when Jack's shot took one of them in the thigh.

"Move." She didn't need to hiss her command twice.

Ducking low, they sprinted for the vacant boundary – the distant blankness which was just a little bit more black than the rest. It was the edge where the desert began, where no living soul would tread during sunrise.

Jack was with her, hand occasionally on her back as if the contact gave them both wings. When she skidded into a messy retreat, she felt the shock of colliding with his body. Heard his warning shout and felt the change in his grip at the same time. There was the shadow of the guard with the intelligence to spot them. They both felt the wrench as they crashed down into the lea of a vast freighter container.

Finch's ears were ringing. It was hard to think. The collision made her head hurt. Sonic weapons were soundless except for the sharp whine on a frequency only bats and dogs could truly hear. She couldn't tell if the whine in her ears was concussion or the weapon fire. And Jack's body was heavy on hers as if he'd shielded her.

It was a frantic struggle to release herself from under him. A crashing relief when he stirred too and shifted enough to save her the job. But he was hurt. He'd taken the hit. And she couldn't see if this was a conventional wound or sonic. She couldn't tell if it was localised. Or if she'd have to watch him decay before her eyes.

She forced down the rising panic with a steady stream of curses. It was either that or sob. Her eyes were frantically searching for the guard. No sign of him. But no time to think either. The snipper would be stalking closer. He'd be cautiously moving to find for a new angle to finish the job. No hope now of crossing that empty space before the boundary.

This jaunt really would go wrong if Jack died. And she'd absolutely *kill* him if the unexpected issue with his papers cost her own life as well.

The weight of his arm was heavy over her shoulders. But she wouldn't let go. Perhaps the sonic weapon didn't always kill. Perhaps there was hope sometimes. She couldn't remember how long it normally took. She gripped his waist and dragged him, forced him to keep moving, snarled at him to keep conscious until they could duck up against the flank of the enemy shuttle. Its range would be less than they needed, but more than enough to clear this cargo hub.

The nearest guards were foolish. They were looking for instruction from the man who must have been the sniper. He was an easy target when he climbed to his feet on top of the freight container – even when firing from her hip.

Inside the shuttle was sparse and made of wipe-clean polymer. It had none of the lumpen soul of her ship.

She dropped Jack hard into the passenger seat. Reached clumsily for the safety harness. Found that he revived enough to claim the fastenings from her hands.

"You with me?" she asked, sliding her hands from beneath his and moving to claim her own seat. She began the engine start with one hand while the other yanked her own harness into place.

"Aye, aye Captain. All the way."

Lights were flashing on the dashboard, not all of

them good. This was going to be a bumpy launch. And a tricky rendezvous – if there was a ship to meet up with at all. Outside, there were an awful lot of arms pointing at the shuttle as the gangway retracted. The engine spluttered. Groaned into life.

"With you to the end."

The quiet addition snatched her head round. His face was a sickly green colour and there was blood on his sleeve. Wonderful, conventional blood. His weary hand lifted to make an airy gesture. "Or whatever fiercely loyal remark I'm supposed to make at this stage of your rescue."

He surprised a bark of a laugh out of her.

"Don't get ahead of yourself," she retorted grimly, and hauled back on the controls. Felt the punch in the gut as the g-force kicked in.

This, she thought, was definitely going to work.

LIFE

DAPHNE DENLEY

Like the oceans that surround us,
    partly undiscovered place
We are yet to know beyond the skies and
    all that's up in space
Life exists between earth's rocks, so in other
    planets too?
Stars of the galaxy creations, that formed the
    me and you
Maybe life is primitive, a tiny speck or blob
Or evolved beyond, so far advanced,
    for eternity belong
No matter how much we feel alone,
    in universe and space
We live in hope or fear we most, superior of race?

SPRING CAME SLOWLY

ANGELA REDDAWAY

Perhaps it might have been more truthful to say that spring, as such, never came at all to *Spherodica.* But there were disturbing changes.

At first, it was not realised. It may have crossed more than one brain among the species existing there that the rimy, rather putrid green mist that rose from the vast lakes – and descended like a sinister marinade on the surface of this moon – did not augur well for the future.

But in the manner of all phenomena, there were doubtless those who, while regarding ashen and wilting life as unfavourable, nonetheless regarded it as containing some kind of beauty. Others, like gurus and prophets, read it as a portent of terminal destruction – which it was.

The most exalted form of life that existed on *Spherodica* was a stunted being. It transported itself in a rhythmic hobbling movement, disturbing perhaps to the gaze of beings familiar only with humanoid symmetry, but nevertheless presenting a spectacle of a deviant concept of charm.

Alugilac was a classic example of the genus, in his

silvery quilt-like carapace, with several tentacles of netted metallic texture emerging from his abdomen and undulating. These pulsating protuberances had evolved gradually and were intended for the equivalent of feeding, excreting and reproductive purposes. The tempo of the surging and swelling of each protrusion indicated its ultimate function.

Organs that provided a combination of seeing and sensing were located loosely in the upper part of the creature's frame, encased in a transparent silica shell. Living suspended freely in an aqueous solution, there were no specific number. Occasionally they would wilt and die, but new ones always took their place. The resulting effect was a glow of iridescent jewel-like distended swellings. In shades of indigo and emerald, they rotated and glistened as they sensed their immediate, distant and remote surroundings. Several of those used for seeing, specialised in specific wavelengths. These ranged from radio, microwave, infra-red, through to ultra-violet and far beyond to gamma wavelengths. Thus, they had observed changes in a planet within their own system.

Alugilac was a classic example of the most desirable qualities of his race. Able to see, hear, think, touch and communicate non-verbally, and even to experience and transmit a cognitive and mild emotional response.

At this time, disturbing changes were being observed with qualms and trepidation among the more intelligent of the moon's population. A cataclysm was truly feared, and the resident populace sensed that before further time elapsed, they would need to find a new moon or planet on which to survive. The aerosphere which supported life for them, would be poisonous for other forms of life. Their aim was to find another heavenly sphere which they could pollute until the existing species died out. Their own immunity would then allow them to inhabit it and make it their own.

As the finest proponent of his breed, Alugilac was selected to investigate the planet, to evaluate its feasibility.

Having assessed it as suitable, his task was to motivate the inhabitants to accommodate an environment more acceptable to those from *Spherodica*, all within a timescale that would allow his own genus to prepare for emigration before their own habitation disintegrated completely.

The inhabitants were amazingly suggestible and Alugilac was able to advance them to the point of self-extermination. Hydrocarbons were extracted, along with ever more toxic chemicals. Radioactive materials were mined and gathered in vast quantities. Mass conflict was suggested and accelerated the processing of the planet's resources. Initial experiments in fusion were successful but caused an unexpected by-product, peace. Alugilac set to influencing emotional and social disruption ready for the final element.

As with the inhabitants of *Spherodica*, there were those who, while regarding the changes in their daily life as unfavourable, nonetheless accepted the decay of their world without question.

The opportunity to complete this transmutation came fortuitously when Man (the resident population of planet Earth), in his desire to conquer further areas of the Universe, decided to send representatives of his species to explore further into space. During the descent back to Earth, the capsule containing the astronauts was successfully contaminated by a meteoric missile of Alugilac's creation. It contained the seed material of his alien moon's atmosphere.

During the next few years, delivery was implanted in a densely populated land and invisibly replicated itself. It developed, as planned, into a wave of illness that would swiftly cause death and panic throughout a world already commencing the process of disintegration.

No one noticed while Alugilac and his race waited patiently for the virus to take its devastating effect.

KISSING BUG

AMARIS CHASE

She woke with a terrible thirst that even water couldn't quench. As she started drinking a third glass of water, she rubbed the side of her neck which felt stiff and sore. She felt two small bumps at the bottom of her neck. An examination in the mirror revealed two tiny angry red spots.

Those damned insects! she thought. The heat brought out whole colonies of those pesky, bloodthirsty cretins.

She splashed water on her face and made herself a fry up breakfast. She just needed something to absorb the aftermath of the drinking session from the night before. She enjoyed the oblivion that drink brought her, where problems could dissolve into nothingness, and pain could be suppressed in a fug of memory loss. She always accepted the consequences the following day. The pain was worth it.

She couldn't remember much of last night, which was always a good sign in her view. Then thirst overtook the hunger. She tried having orange juice and coffee with her breakfast, but the thirst continued to rage! Her breakfast wasn't having a its usual therapeutic effect. She felt no energy and craved black pudding. She then made a protein shake but nearly brought it back up. She felt weak and lethargic, and the thirst began to dominate her being. Then all of a sudden, the thirst changed to a craving for raw meat and blood. Succulent, stringy meat oozing with fresh blood ...

Could she be pregnant and having a strange craving? She was certain she wasn't. Perhaps this was a new side effect of her monthly cycle, where the loss of blood made you crave blood? Did that ever happen? Whatever the reason, her lust for fresh blood now consumed her so much that she was ready to sink her teeth into a live cow.

She checked the time: it was past midday. The local Japanese restaurant would open soon where she could have an order of sashimi and fulfil her craving for raw meat and not come across as being odd. She was sure some raw beef would make her feel more human. If only she knew the irony of her thoughts ...

She grabbed her keys and ignored her cat lest it fall victim to her inhuman urges. As she stepped outside, the sun scorched her skin and stung her eyes.

In her doorway, a tiny bug observed her with amusement. Its official name was *Triatiminae,* a commonly known as the 'kissing bug, 'bloodsucker' or 'vampire bug'.

Little did this innocuous bug realise that it had only days before bitten into the flesh of a reptilian alien masquerading as a human. The bug had transferred alien genes into this lady who was now displaying the reptilian urge for raw meat.

And little did the aliens realise that this would be the fastest way to conquer the human population.

SPACE DESTINATION UNKNOWN

BEVERLEY GORDON

I found myself wandering through space
        searching for a place to rest
I came across a little planet called earth,
        I decided to investigate
Its occupants were far too violent for me
So I set about the galaxy once more, avoiding the
        notorious meteorites
Large and small as they approached with great speed,
        I tried to avoid them
I turned my craft Space Atlanta in a panic that sent it
        out of control
A piece of meteor got lodged in one of
        Space Atlanta's engines

Is this the end of me I wondered as I went into an
        uncontrollable spin.
Not likely.
Death is not in my plan. I somehow manage to get
        Space Atlanta steady

Where I am, I do not know – this old technology
needs to go
But where in space can I find new parts
I am running on two engines here, I am lost in space
Facing the danger of not returning home

How did I get myself in this position you might ask
I come from a small underground planet that is within
the planet you know so well
But out of reach
I used to watch the earth people land their spacecraft
and hang a cloth on a stick
I watch as they bounce about like my uncle Jack in his
space box
I have a simple job and that is to keep my planet clean
But a mind of an engineer is built in me
When the earth people leave their junk behind
I made great use for them
I design my craft Space Atlanta but it got rejected,
that's what I thought
Now I see I was tricked. My people wanted to
invade earth
We have the technology to see that the earth people
are not looking after their planet
I did not mean to push the button. I heard a noise
so I jumped back
So here I am looking for a way back home before
they awaken

As I wander about in space, navigating my way
through the galaxies
Not knowing where I am or where I am heading, my
Space Alanta needs repairing
What was that? My Space Atlanta has come to a stop
I open the door what a surprise. I am attached to what
seems like a giant spaceship
But there is no one about. I tread cautiously
Not knowing what danger I am about to face
As I slowly move around the ship
I have never seen anything like it
Strange food, plant that grow in cool boxes
What is this funny shape object, soft and bouncy?
All of a sudden I hear voices – I hide. But where?

I cannot tell you for I am more than the eyes can see

A tall figure comes in, what is that? The head comes
off the outer body
Oh it's a human … it has two skins, that is strange
The human lays down on that funny object, then
presses a button
And more humans appear in a box as I keep quiet
and observe the strange goings on of this
human. Could it be possible I was mistaken
about the humans?
But I came to their planet and got my spacecraft
shot at.
While I look for parts for my Space Atlanta I will
observe this human even more

Maybe I can save their planet from their
own destruction
Or my people will invade.
I needed to return to my people with evidence,
in the hope that they will
Give the humans time to repair their planet

But will this human trust me? I need to get to
know it, but how? I will continue to observe it
In the meantime, I must repair my Space Atlanta
in secret.

CHEAP TRIP ABROAD

MYLES CUTLER

My parents were having a go at me again. It had gone way beyond cautious questioning and oblique enquiries. Now it was *"Where are the kids?" "What are you doing with your life?" "What happened to those nice brothers who used to take you out?" "Didn't you like one of them? You only need to like one"*. I said that I knew where babies came from, that I had to go, and cut the call.

I connected to my best friend. I could hear her kids squeaking in the background while she listened to me.

"I feel like I haven't achieved anything," I said. "Yet I don't even know what it is that I want to achieve. Having children wouldn't help; even if I could find some males I liked."

My friend thought for a moment then came back. "You need some perspective, some distance. How about a trip away? Flights are cheap at the moment."

"With you?" I said excitedly.

"No," she said "the kids are at that funny age. I think they could be beginning to split. Listen, choose somewhere remote, undeveloped where you'll have time to think and reflect. Maybe you'll even find a new direction."

Each day after work (and sometimes during work) I scanned the holiday listings but found nothing that seemed to offer any chance of 'me' time. I was getting slightly desperate because it was only a few weeks from Mother's Day and I knew my parents would expect me to visit and stay for while. Plus I would also have to visit aunties, uncles, cousins, and nieces too whilst I was there. It wasn't that I didn't love them but, my friend was right, I needed to get away. Then I found it: a new destination just opened up to tourists. It was a poor place and basic but hot, cheap, and not crowded with visitors or attractions.

I booked for a month but the company would only hold it provisionally until I'd had the three different types of vaccinations required. At the Travel Medical Centre, the supervisor looked at my destination and asked "Are you sure? That place is not developed at all."

I said that it was fine and it was where I wanted to go.

The vaccines were new, expensive, and powerful and I didn't feel great for a few days afterwards. I perked up though when the holiday company confirmed my booking. I connected to my parents and said awkwardly that I wouldn't be home for Mother's Day. They were surprisingly unfussed; pleased even. Perhaps they thought I would meet some partners. I kept my destination vague; I didn't want to worry them.

Now I was on a trip. A trip to get away from my job, my extended family; the environment back home. I needed to refresh my spirits, reset my values, and find myself again. The flight was long but we stopped off frequently and, as usual with these cheap trips, we had to get local transport to our final downstream destination.

When we landed, the sky was clear blue and we disembarked through a half-empty dusty terminal. Outside there were rows of ancient taxis. I had the name of my hotel written down in their language and showed it to nearest driver. He nodded, stowed my luggage, and then opened the rear door for me. I got in and sat in the chilled air.

We started off and I watched the scenery passing: a brown, arid landscape full of ruins. Some of them open to the sky like dead sea creatures: the contents long gone, just the shell left. Others like square spires, sometimes two or three together, jagged at the tops like huge corroded spikes. Now and again I felt the taxi driver watching me in the rear-view mirror. If I looked he would snap back to the road, concentrating hard.

I checked into the hotel. It was threadbare but free of the dust outside and had chilled air. The bed was not right but they moved me to a different room without question. The staff had a kind of deference, almost humility, like they were trying to make up for something they had done wrong. Over the course of the holiday I would encounter this over and over again.

For the next three weeks I travelled widely; almost

always with the taxi driver I had met at the terminal. Once he took me to see his family. The children squealed and backed away when they saw me. He admonished them and they came back shyly; staring at me. They probably hadn't seen anyone of my colour or in my type of clothes before. The whole family lived in two rooms in part of a ruin. There were solar panels fixed to the outside walls and an old air conditioner was rattling in a corner. The man's wife offered me some food. I picked at it carefully, not wanting to offend but on the other hand I didn't even recognise some of the things on the plate. They could have been decoration for all I knew. I tried my translation app but the local dialect was beyond it (in fact I found out later that someone from the northern half of the place wouldn't understand someone from the southern half).

I pondered about the people here. I wondered what they thought about us coming to visit them, to watch them in their poverty. Yet there was an eagerness in them to start again, to learn, to try. I thought about what I had at home and looked at what they had here and felt ashamed. They had so little but kept going. My 'worries' were nothing in comparison and in that moment I decided to stay and help. I got in contact with my Embassy and they arranged for me to join the Interplanetary League for the Assistance of Planet Earth.

THE SPACE BETWEEN US

JANE PHILLIPS

There was a time we two were seen as one,
Always together, doing the same things,
Close-coupled and in tune
Living life to the full
It all was fun.

As time went by, the space between us
Moon-like, waxed and waned.
Each had new interests, new aims,
New places to explore,
New friends, beliefs, opinions.

The space between us grew and grew.
At first it was ignored,
Too insignificant to matter
(So it seemed).
But now we seldom meet,
And when we do, I have to bite my tongue,
To silence all the things that I could say,
Relieved, my friend, you live so far away!

STARNIGHT

AMANDA JANE DAVIES

Standing in the hallway with her parents, sixteen-year-old Bronwyn James buttoned up her suede coat over her long-sleeved top and jeans. The only light source was what filtered through the door and windows from the moon and myriad stars. Outside would be chilly, and as the westerly winds picked up, her father unlocked the front door.

Quickly, she zipped up her boots, feeling safer wearing her favourite clothes. The sirens sounded and in the gloom they caught each other's eyes, followed by their hands, as they walked wordlessly into the street to join their neighbours for *Starnight*.

It was expected. This mass gathering. Long-held traditions and religious holidays had been abandoned decades ago. Nowadays gatherings only happened on the winter solstice, when everyone made a wish upon the stars. The same night that, two hundred years ago, new-world-rules began.

Bronwyn walked in an almost hypnotic trance,

oblivious to the harsh wind that blasted her face and fingers. Her feet in step with her family, her mind occupied by what would happen in the next few minutes. She thought Starnight wasn't something to be celebrated like the authorities told people to do. Because after wishing, she, like everybody else, would fall asleep after feasting and awake infected with new diseases. This madness had to stop.

"Hello Mr and Mrs James. Hello Bronwyn," said Rhys, their neighbour. He lowered his voice, "They'll be here in the morning – those pseudo-humans – to hand out their curing food boxes. Didn't stop my wife dying, did they? Nor my son Elwyn's disappearance. What were our leaders thinking when they signed that peace and participation agreement?"

"It was the only way to end the interplanetary war," said Mr James.

"A war we should have avoided," snarled Rhys. "We gave them too much power and now we have to wear their life-controlling wristbands."

Bronwyn rubbed at her wristband in part an act of comfort and part an act of hate. The kinetic energy lightbulb that normally allowed her to see the remaining time left on it in the dark was automatically disabled. All artificial sources of illumination were switched off tonight. Not just here, but across the last of the land. There was only one continent now, covering a tiny part of Earth. The rest vast ocean.

"Look at that army patrolling the street. We know using unnatural light tonight results in instant death.

Do they have to make it so obvious?" whispered Bronwyn.

"This is 2503. Are you ready for wishing?" erupted a female voice from out of the sky.

"Affirmative," came a human reply from a control room underground.

"Begin wishing."

Bronwyn felt it. They said you couldn't, but she did. For a second an intense heat surged through her body, then it was gone. She looked at the sky – the moon had disappeared. She saw the stars rushing towards her, then nothing except blackness as their luminescence faded too. This was the bit that Bronwyn dreaded – the feeling that light would never return.

The crowd fell silent, fervently waiting for the galaxy brightness to return. Bronwyn knew when that happened, she'd also know the outcome of her wish. She'd feel it in her belly and bones.

As the moon and stars reappeared people became animated. Her dad laughing and cheering, her mother tearful. A few remained silent like Rhys. Unnervingly, he screamed and turned a flashlight onto himself; before Bronwyn could react to cover this terrible breach of the taboo, he dropped dead at her feet. Soldiers swooped in pushing people out of the way. They hoisted Rhys up and took him away.

Shivering with disgust at the bullet's rapid destruction, Bronwyn and her family returned home. They had become almost immune to the depths of cruelty inflicted by the army. So, after briefly grieving and reminiscing they took comfort in feasting on their homecooked foods. Taking time to enjoy their suppers because by morning everything would change.

Climbing into bed Bronwyn wondered if her parents' wishes would come true. She suspected they had both wished for the same thing – a boy – to replace the son who had died a year before.

Bronwyn secretly disapproved of their wish. Not because she didn't want her parents to be happy but because she didn't think she could face losing another brother like the way she lost Gethin. It had broken her heart. She'd idolised her older brother. He'd been intelligent and popular. Though more importantly: he had been good to her. The type of brother that had taught her to climb trees, build camps and laugh at her dismal jokes. He would have made a fine man.

In her exhaustion, Bronwyn reiterated her unspoken promise to her brother, "Gethin, I will do everything in my power to help stop these Starnight experiments from killing any more people. Even if it means putting my own life at risk."

She'd have to finish what he'd started if she was to find any kind of solace. After all, he'd taught her everything he knew about the army. He'd said he knew why they were really here and their future intent for humankind. She'd listened intently as he lay delirious, whispering on his deathbed. Making her promise to never tell her parents or anyone else.

Her head began to pound. It was the start of several symptoms and conditions that would affect everyone for several weeks. It was the only time humans were ever ill. Gradually, after eating the supplied food everybody, mostly, returned to their normal selves. In exchange for a few weeks illness the 'stars' generally granted their wish.

When she was six Bronwyn thought wishes only lasted a year, but upon questioning her father she understood that you were granted it for the first year, then after that it was up to you to keep your wish alive.

He'd said, "smaller wishes were always granted. However, bigger ones come at a cost."

As she got older he also warned her to "never wish for the impossible, like Starnight ending, as it would only result in her death."

Bronwyn was ten when she became eligible to make her first wish. The same year as she got her Life wristband. From that day forward everything she did would result in seconds added or subtracted from her life. The army put it on her, and there was no way to take it off.

She'd been scared, going to the chamber underground. Fake people in white coats, sitting her on a hard metal chair, bolted to the floor. Gethin had walked her there. A day with grey skies and misty rain. She remembered their conversation moments before she was ushered in.

"Does it hurt when they put it on?"

"No. It's just like wearing a watch."

"But you can't take it off? Ever?"

"No. It has no clasp. Once it's on it sort of shrinks

so you can't slide it off either. It becomes part of your skin."

"Like a tattoo? Is it organic?"

He'd laughed and replied, "Honestly, sis, I don't know."

Drifting into sleep, she wondered how come nobody had noticed the time rapidly decreasing on Gethin's wristband until it was too late. What had he done to reduce his lifespan so quickly? What hadn't he told her?

Feeling nauseous the next morning, Bronwyn took her food box from the army official at the front door and shouted to her parents fetch theirs. Her head was pounding but she knew it would be better to try and eat. As she slowly licked some paste, she thought back to the last normal conversation between her and her brother. "Gethin, why are the food boxes important?"

"I think the cures are in them," he'd replied.

"But there's no rule to say you have to eat the food. You can give your food to someone else if they're hungry. The only rule is you take your own box from the man and then when its empty to the recycling centre once you're better.

"Stop looking for trouble Bronwyn."

"But everyone has to go to the recycling centre. Unless they're dead. We know the deceased's food box is collected by the army. They examine the body, then take it and the box away. You must have some idea why"

"I think we recover by touching the box rather than eating the food," Gethin said.

That year she had studied her box, and his, but

they seemed exactly the same. They were large, metal, lightweight and cool to touch. They didn't warm in your hands like other metals. They were solid. She had kicked them, jumped on them, sat on them, and even tried to scratch them with a compass. Absolutely nothing damaged them. In frustration she had spat in one, hoping to learn something new. She'd been careful though – many people had lost their lives questioning Starnight rituals.

Gethin had died a week after Starnight. After she'd recovered from some kind of flu, her grief had turned to anger. Once quiet and polite, her parents struggled to reason with her. She knew she was making them unhappy, but she wanted them to hate her. Needed them to – because she knew it was her fault Gethin's time had elapsed. She shouldn't have encouraged him in his quest for answers. She shouldn't have asked him to tell her what he'd learned. She should've told her parents, and she definitely shouldn't have told Rhys that she thought his son Elwyn's disappearance two years ago and Gethin's death last year were linked. But she had.

Back in bed Bronwyn recalled how instead of paying attention at school she'd sought out Gethin's friends and discovered people who, like her, wanted change. She'd began leading a double life – the underachieving, grieving sister, and the determined sassy young woman who wanted to end Starnight misery for ever.

Her parents would kill her if they knew she associated with these people. That is, if the army didn't do it first. So this Starnight she'd been careful to wish for something small. She needed more answers so had wished for a dog. She hoped walking a dog would give her a reason to be out every evening after school. And by going out she could secretly meet these likeminded people.

A WEEK LATER

Bronwyn's parents were in high spirits, acting like teenagers. Her dog had arrived an hour ago and she hated that there was a curfew tying her to the house for another week while people recovered.

She wondered who'd experienced the despair of un-granted wishes. Once you'd asked for something you could never wish for it again. As a small child she had never understood this as both her and Gethin had been wished for. Now she understood her parents had wished first for a son then later a daughter. What had they wished for now? A hermaphrodite?

"Mum, have you and dad wished for a child?" she asked hesitantly.

"You know I can't tell you," her mother replied.

Sighing, she took her dog to her bedroom and told it everything she knew. Then she began to make plans, mapping out walking routes where she could safely meet others without the army's prying eyes.

SIX MONTHS LATER

Bronwyn walked her dog to the secret meeting place. It was getting dark, so they had little time to spare. Once the street lights came on, no one was allowed outside. Another stupid rule.

"We found this in Rhys's house," said John – his brother – to the group, holding up a mini projector. "The data drive is still in it. It contains a film of what happened to his son two years ago."

Bronwyn braced herself, she knew she had to watch it, but it wouldn't be easy. An image appeared showing a steel room containing a metal bed screwed to the wall and a swivel chair bolted to the floor.

A woman sat on the chair watching Elwyn's wristband count down his remaining life minutes. He lay helpless on the bed sobbing. "Please," he begged in desperation, "please can you give me more time?"

She shook her head and said in a venomous voice, "No Elwyn, there is nothing I can do."

"You bitch!" he yelled.

She let go of his wrist shoving it away from her. "Thank you Elwyn. Leave me with hate why don't you."

Swiveling she turned away from him, seemingly unwilling to witness his final three seconds.

Oh My Days, thought Bronwyn, that's the voice from the sky. That woman is 2503.

"I'm sorry I wished to meet you," whispered Elwyn. Then the long beep from his wristband indicated he had died.

2503 deactivated his wristband and let herself out of the room. CCTV cameras followed her as she walked to the control office where an old man was waiting.

"Did he say anything?"

"He just said he wished we hadn't met, Father."

"Humppphhh."

2503 went to her dashboard and opened a database. She found Elwyn's record and ticked the cell marked deceased.

The film stopped and John said, "I don't know how Rhys got hold of this. I think maybe Gethin was involved, he was very technically minded … and maybe that's why he died. Probably Rhys turned on that flashlight because he'd seen Elwyn dying and realised he was responsible for Gethin's death too. He couldn't bear to go through another Starnight pretending to everyone everything was okay."

"What do you mean?" asked an older lady sitting next to Bronwyn.

"That woman's job is to subtract life time from us. It's a business. The company's called LifeForce, you can see it on their uniform."

"Did you notice the wristbands?" asked Bronwyn, "Elwyn's had nearly twenty minutes on it, but when he called her a bitch, she took nineteen of them and added them to her own."

John played the film again, to see it for himself, and what else they might have missed.

"Oh hell," he groaned. "Look down the list from Elwyn's name. I'm so sorry," he said, staring at Bronwyn.

She studied the image then looked at her wristband. Earlier it had shown ninety years, now it showed twenty-four hours. She remembered reading her mother's diary where her mum had written that she'd wished for twins. In her father's diary she'd read he'd asked for a child to replace that which was lost. She put her head in her hands and tried not to cry as she realised the power of their combined wish.

Then she thought of something and said "John, please play the film again."

She and her dog had just entered her parents' house when she felt it again – that intense heat of the wishing. Suddenly 2503 was speaking in the hallway air. "Bronwyn James, what have you got to say for yourself? It's past curfew, you should have been in ten minutes ago. Well? Speak?"

"I want you to go. You, Starnight and your stupid army!"

"Be careful, I can end your life right now."

"Yeah, well it's over anyway, isn't it? Why prolong the agony?"

"You should be afraid."

"Well I'm not. You can't kill me if I'm not wearing my wristband. And you can't kill my friends when they're not wearing theirs either."

She rushed to both her parents, who stood open-mouthed by the stairs.

"I saw it," she blurted to them. "Rhys's film. No time to explain."

She grabbed their wrists and replaying the recording of the voice of 2503, said, "Wish Deactivation. Unclip!"

The wristbands fell to the floor, disintegrating. "Mum, Dad, there's a rebellion! Soon we'll be free."

BEYOND SELENE

ANDREW LAZENBY

The cow jumped over the moon, but where
did they land?

So what's there, is anyone out there …
I don't want to know … or do I?
Mysteries to be solved or just rings to unravel.

Intelligence, Intelligent forms
I wonder, can they decide what to call themselves
Or is that just us?

Will I ever know, each year we get a bit more
of a peek,
A bit more detail, a bit more colour,
We get a little bit closer and a little bit farther away
(comparatively speaking).

In general, overall, taking all things into account,
I would say we are oblivious

I worry about all the junk that is already out there
Space junk, the galaxy equivalent of our plastic bags
and discarded shopping trolleys

The big questions:
Can space be divided,
Can space be controlled,
Can space be defined,
Can space grow,
Is space on a journey?

How can we understand the brilliance of the stars,
... The milky way,
... The black hole,
... Cosmic voids

Space, almost within our reach, yet so far beyond
our comprehension

Are the sun and the moon about the same size?

THE FINAL FRONTIER

MICHAEL BARTLETT

Another day, another solar system. Another week, another galaxy. I won't give in to despair but there are times when I lie awake wondering if our journey will ever end. As the Senior Sentient Being (SSB) of this odyssey I feel the responsibility very personally. Will we ever find a place to settle and create a new life for our community or have we just exchanged one disaster for another?

At the time it seemed we had no choice. We were – well, still are – a society of shape-shifters. Our body chemistry allows us to assume a variety of different forms according to the need of the moment. We did not choose this ability, we were born with it and, I suppose, we took it for granted.

Maybe we became arrogant. Over time our species made huge advances in technology but we were never satisfied and so we created more and more machines and devices to take over most of the functions of our existence. However, somewhere along the line this expanding technology escaped our control and the machines that were created to serve us began to control us instead. The technical innovations became wilder and wilder. Our planet was no longer a place of freedom but a rapidly escalating technological dictatorship heading for disaster.

At first many of us didn't notice what was happening but gradually we realised that our free will had been eroded, especially our ability to shape-shift. This was fundamental to our existence and without it we effectively became a slave culture.

However, the takeover wasn't total. Those who worked in the space station that orbited our planet realised that the power of the machines did not apply outside our atmosphere. On the space station we could still shape-shift at will but once back on the planet's surface that ability left us again and we were fixed in whatever shape and personality we had currently adopted.

However, this discovery offered a glimmer of hope so a number of us Sentient Beings got together and decided to plan for a different future. We realised that to regain our freedom we would have to leave our home planet but at the same time we could not simply move elsewhere in our own solar system as ours was the only place with the right balance of atmosphere and natural resources that could support our form of life. The conclusion was therefore inevitable. We had to travel out into deep space, to try and find another home, but to do that we needed a completely new type of vessel.

To be honest, I don't know how we managed to achieve this but achieve it we did. The vessel that we built – and in which are now travelling – was built on the space station in orbit. The design team were brilliant. As our future was completely unknown they came up with a wonderful concept. They adapted the basic chemistry that allowed us Sentient Beings to shape-shift so that it would also work with inanimate materials.

Even I don't really understand all the technical details but to put it simply they created a space vessel which could also shape-shift so it could be made to suit whatever circumstances we might encounter. However, once it enters an atmosphere its shape becomes fixed, as do ours, so when we're approaching a new planet which might provide us with a home we have to take a lot of instant decisions, based on very little information, about what form we each need to assume.

Not easy to get it right. Very easy to get it wrong.

Once the vessel was ready we set off. Because I am a scientist, specifically a cosmologist, I had been elected Senior Sentient Being (SSB) and so, for better or worse, I became responsible for this vessel and its passengers. There were several hundred of us on board and once free of the planet's atmosphere we all adopted the shape in which we felt most comfortable. We were certainly a mixed bag.

We left our solar system and entered the world of deep space. We passed through endless galaxies, explored different solar systems, always seeking for a planet somewhere with the right factors to allow us to settle down and rebuild our lives.

Measuring time in deep space is not easy as you have no point of reference so I cannot say exactly when it was that our instruments recorded the huge explosion. We certainly felt the shock waves and when we examined our star maps we realised it was our own home planet which had finally overreached itself and had imploded. We had escaped, we were alive, but did we have a future?

It is hard to say how long and how far we have travelled. Periodically we have to land somewhere, even if we don't intend to stay, as we have to recharge our energy banks and that can only be done using the power of a sun. Mostly we land on a suitable planet, stay for around ten sleeps to recharge our vessel and then we are on our way again.

We always do an analysis before landing to see if this particular planet might be suitable for our permanent home. Usually there was something that made it impossible but twice our hopes were raised but it was not to be.

There was one planet where we landed on what seemed like a vast open plain. The atmosphere was suitable, the climate seemed right, the terrain seemed unoccupied. This is important as we do not want to invade an existing culture. On this occasion we chose to make our vessel into a giant circular shape but unfortunately the moment we touched down we began to sink into what seemed to be glutinous mud. We put on full power but for a moment the suction held us before we managed to pull free and head back into the sky.

That was a disappointment but our next attempt was worse. Once again, in yet another solar system, we identified a planet that seemed suitable. Our instruments showed no sign of life so we turned our vessel into the shape of a long thin cylinder and we came slowly in to land. The touchdown was successful, our instruments showed that we could breathe the air and for a moment we really felt we had arrived.

However, when we lifted the shields and peered out we saw a huge herd of monstrous creatures charging over the ground towards us. They appeared to be very much larger than us, each one had eight lower appendages and several long horns protruding from their upper body. It was clear that their intentions were not peaceful, so without more ado we put on power and took off again. Very disappointing.

And now, yet again, I am faced with a decision. Our vessel's energy levels are very low so it is essential that we land somewhere in the very near future. I scanned our star maps and spotted a tiny planet in a small solar system in the spiral arm of a nearby galaxy. It didn't look very promising but it appeared to be about the right distance from their sun and when your power source is beginning to run dry you have very little choice so I entered its coordinates and we headed for it.

As we approached I made the usual announcement to my fellow Sentient Beings. Basically, I tell them we are about to touch down again to recharge our energy banks and I remind them to choose a shape they will be comfortable with while this is happening as our shape shifting ability will cease once we enter the planet's atmosphere.

I have a preferred shape for myself on these occasions, one which I find most comfortable. Basically I have two protuberances which support my main body, a further two similar, but smaller, protuberances extend from the upper part of my body and my brain container is perched on top of the lot. The only slight irritation is the amount of hair which hangs down from the bottom of my brain container but I guess nothing's perfect.

Once everyone was ready I guided our vessel into the planet's orbit and made preparations for landing. However, as we got closer I had a shock, something our instruments had failed to indicate. When we did a complete visual circuit of the planet we realised that it appeared to be entirely covered by water, there was no indication of solid land anywhere. This was a nuisance, but as all we wanted to do was to recharge our power supply it was not insurmountable. I adapted the shape of our vessel so that it would float on water and down we went.

We landed with a bit of a splash and then drifted there on this vast ocean. The atmosphere was breathable, the temperature was comfortable, so I opened the main doors so my fellow Sentient Beings could go outside the hull. Meanwhile I began the recharging process.

Several sleeps later we were still there, bobbing about on the water in a gentle motion that was actually quite comforting. The recharging was almost complete and I began making preparations to take off again when one of our Sentient Beings, whose speciality happened to be astronomy, came to me with an interesting observation.

"I don't think being entirely covered by water is the natural state of this planet," the astronomy SB said.

"What makes you think that?"

"Since we have been here I've been taking regular star sights and they appear to be moving. That's unlikely so I think if it's not the stars that are changing it must be us. I think we're sinking."

"Sinking?"

"Not literally, obviously, but I think the water level below us is less than it was when we arrived."

"So what you're saying is…."

"…that there may be firm ground somewhere below us. I'm wondering if perhaps there was some kind of natural disaster here a while back and it's now begun to revert to normal."

That gave me food for thought. This planet was ideal for us in so many ways if only it wasn't entirely covered by water. If the water level really was falling and there was solid land below us, might this finally be the place where we could settle?

I called a council meeting as we all had to agree on any form of action. I gave them the facts and suggested that we stayed here for a while longer to see if the water continued to recede. If it did, and if we could find solid land somewhere, then maybe we could think of making a home here.

Everyone was as tired of the constant search as I was but some – especially those who knew nothing about astronomy – asked if there were some way we confirm if firm ground really did exist below the water.

I could not see how this was possible but then two of our Sentient Beings offered to go and explore. As it happens, the body forms they had chosen before we landed was that of amphibians so they said they would swim out from our ship and see what they could find.

This offer was gratefully accepted and they set off. They were gone some while but when they returned one of them was carrying a short length of what looked like withy in its mouth.

"We found this plant-like growth poking out of the water and brought this back to show you. It was wet, so maybe it was covered by water until fairly recently. We can go back later and see if any more has been exposed."

Two sleeps later they returned with the news that a lot more of the plant-like growth was now above the water.

"And this time there were fronds on it. See?" And they handed over a green frond still attached to a withy.

From this expedition it was clear that the water level was decreasing so the 'wait and see' suggestion was passed unanimously.

I did point out that if we did stay here then everyone was committed to the shape they had chosen before we left orbit as we didn't have shape shifting ability within the planet's atmosphere. That was clearly understood and accepted.

The astronomy SB continued the star observations, the amphibian SBs made further expeditions and gradually we realised that our optimism was justified. More and more land appeared until finally our vessel was floating in a kind of lake with solid land all around. Before long even the lake had disappeared and our ship was resting on the soil

We held another meeting and it was agreed unanimously that we should stay on this planet and try and create a new community. Maybe this time we could get it right. Gradually our Sentient Beings in their various forms began leaving our vessel, walking, hopping, trotting, sliding, flapping, heading off into the unknown to start a new life.

I watched them go. I know it was chance that brought us here but somehow I felt a great sense of achievement. Then, as I looked out upon this new landscape, I suddenly saw a renboga, that's the effect that comes when the reflection, refraction and dispersion of light in water droplets results in a spectrum of light appearing in the sky.

It was beautiful and somehow it filled me with hope.

PLAYTHING

REBECCA MCDOWALL

Saturdays. Leopold's favourite day of the week. When he had first arrived on Earth, he had designated Saturdays as his day to subtly play with humans, humans were his favourite pet. Easy to manipulate – in a harmless, not going to break anything, but if you realise what I'm doing your mind may melt sort of way.

It had taken him almost a decade to choose just how he was going to play with them. For the first seven years, he had debated keeping some as house pets, just like he'd seen the older humans do with their little ones. However, whenever he tried to employ one of the mankind tradesmen to build him a cage they quickly disappeared. Clearly, humans were not caged pets. He'd have to get a bunny at some point.

It was during a rather dull mid-morning stroll around the local botanical garden that Leopold happened to overhear two of the little humans discussing 'shooting stars'. Fireworks practically exploded out his earholes with excitement. Oh, the fun he was going to have! The ever-expanding universe was a widely accepted concept among mankind, he'd read enough library books in his last few years here to be up to date on their silly little theories. Generations had watched images projected back to Earth from the myriad of satellites and rovers that had been sent up to explore the dark expanse. The humans had sat, glued to their little screens, avidly soaking up the pictures of 'deep' space. The tiny glimpse of exploding suns, the captivating beauty of the rings that surrounded multiple planets in a multitude of systems. So easily fooled. The conversation he had heard that morning had sparked a whole new game for his pets.

Leopold sat in his shed scanning through his latest downloads. His violet hair had an almost shimmer in the morning sunrise. It always caused a stir when he was out and about. The images brought a smirk to his thin lips. Saturdays did really make being stuck on Earth worth it. Each downloaded file contained a shot of the darkness of space with a small blue whirl in a different section. Subtle but noticeable nonetheless, and completely worthless. The smudge of blue was bright enough to demand the eye's attention. Just enough to captivate the human's intrigue. More than enough to perk the interests of all relevant agencies without a doubt. They always lapped up whatever he sent them. NASA would do its usual routine of examining it and as always eventually authenticating the images but with no explanation as to what they could be showing. The newspapers would run the usual We Are Not Alone feature, posting multiple theories as to what the camera could have captured on film. He often pondered how much NASA would kick themselves when they eventually decided to admit to mankind that they indeed were not alone, that they had reached out to the other lifeforms multiple times but not one lifeform had replied. To let the news run with it was a mistake. They would learn that in time. He would enjoy watching that one play out, maybe he'd get the ball rolling on that one in a few Saturdays.

Bringing the printouts closer to his star-kissed eyes he examined the blue whirl on each one. Idiots, he chuckled to no one in particular. He should have known. It was a distorted hand waving. Brett, he would wager. It was the sort of absolutely first-century behaviour of a youngling that he had come to expect from him. Brett wasn't the only one. They had started taking out the satellite feeds decades ago and replacing them with their own images. Originally, they carried on providing the humans with the bog-standard images that their own technology had been relaying. That had got a little mundane. He wasn't too sure who had been the first to suggest tampering with the images to see how long it would be before the human public would catch on to what was right before them. Bets were on for how quickly they might accept the truth, and then see what the collective actions would be. Leopold personally expected there would be hell to pay in most countries. Humanity was an unusually violent breed – this was the deciding factor that had caused the alien races to ignore humanity's repeated attempts to interact with them.

Stuffing the envelopes addressed to NASA Chiefs with the file prints, he pressed his signature stamp firmly onto the paper. Before repeating the process again for the press copies. He couldn't wait for the eventual fallout. It was his favourite thing about humankind, they never did exactly what you expected them to. That was the one predictable thing about them, the unexpected.

Dusk.

He smiled at his code name. Every time he sent a photo drop, he wished to be a fly on the wall. Humans really were his favourite plaything.

THEY SAY

HOLLY CRAWFORD

They say 'reach for the stars',
When all I want to stretch for is another drink:
Cancel the present
Drown out the past
And I find that, at least, is within my reach

With every gulp of mind-numbing juice,
I get to wondering:
If aliens threw down a scatter of stars
Forming a ladder to whisk me away to Pluto or Mars
(I am old-school and believe the former to still
　　be a planet –
Don't worry Pluto, your supporters remain,)

Would I refuse the chance to start again?
Have my memory wiped
To begin a new (milky) way of life
A galaxy or more away from the multitude of
Mistakes I have managed to make on earth?
I believe I would

Others have 'got this' or are 'smashing that'
Such confidence in their untangled minds
Pathways cleared for success
Meanwhile, my road to sobriety is blocked
Mainly by the labels people throw at me like crumbs
'Loser'. 'Drunk'. 'Waste-Of-Space'.

I've never reached my potential –
Am an outstanding underachiever
Never believed in myself
And nobody has ever successfully dissuaded me of
the notion:
So much easier to take another drink
(I am an expert in getting to the bottom of bottles in
double quick time,
Never find the answers there though, mind.)
Wonderland logic tells me it's better not think
That's the point
Can't take life on life's terms
Maybe I'm an excellent example of how not to live

What not to do?

Frustration burns
At what might have been
Laying where my legs dropped me
Unable to go on with so much vodka inside of me
In a field of grass kissed silver by the moon
I urge, no, *long* for the clouds to pass
Giving way to miles of sky
Laid out like material in a tailor's shop
So much potential, me and the material
So much potential, so much waste
More than anyone could ever see in a lifetime

The outdoor darkness,
Night's darkness has never scared me
The depths of the darkness in my soul
Now that strikes a fear into my being
My bones:

The uncharted pits of despair
That self-destruct button in my head
Just itching to be pressed
Capable and willing to destroy everything for
 one more drink
Not caring for others
Or beyond where my next fix is coming from
So unlike me,
The daytime me, who gets up and dressed
And goes to work all smiles and 'I'm fine's
Whenever a question is posed

So different from the night time me,
But that is the Hyde to my Jekyll
Some things are best left alone

Any yet –
If someone had extended an ounce of kindness
to the Mr,
Would he have changed, become a better man?
After all, nobody is one hundred percent bad.
Should we reach out our hands when and while
we can,
To care for others? I would have cared for him.
Got him counselling or something.
A kind hand on his.

"Aliens, come for me now!"
I holler as the alcohol leaves my veins
No, I am not drunk now
But high on possibilities
I do not hate myself so much sober
Sometimes, I can even see chinks of light
Bits I like about myself
Before loathing tramples them to dust

"I am the one you are looking for
You will never, in all of your searching,
Find someone as fascinating as me to study!"
At last, a glimpse of self-belief!
I am suddenly the second Mrs de Winter
In the latter chapters of Rebecca
Never to be so innocent again

It's gone forever

I believed when there was no evidence
When others laughed and scoffed
Yet now, it has paid off

I squint as the clouds part
Silently they have come
My lift is here, at last
A fresh chance and
The adventure starts …

MOON TREES

AMARIS CHASE

Larissa fingered the tarot deck in her pocket and tried to tune into their energy. The light was fading fast, the sun hung low like a great orb transmitting waves of pinks and purples in the autumn sky.

She preferred to walk through the pinewood at dusk when there were less people about. The village locals preferred to stay away from the woods at night, sensing there was something uncanny about them when they were cloaked in darkness with only the moon to catch their silhouette with silver light. But to Larissa, the trees came alive at night.

Larissa's cottage was at the edge of the woods, where she had grown up traversing the hills and woods around her, taking in the luscious smell of pine in the damp air, using pine needles in her medicines. She frequented the woods so much that on a moonless night she could feel her way through the woods from the touch of the bark on each tree, knowing every crevice and nodule intimately, the mud patches that swelled in the darker corners of the forest, and by the sound of the stream and the feel of the moss underfoot.

She dismissed the superstitions of the villagers, who just didn't understand the power of nature. They whispered about her too after all. The crazy white witch in the village, making herbal potions, hugging trees and reading the tarot. Yet some of these same people would visit her clandestinely, asking for herbal medicines where mainstream science failed, or guidance through the tarot. These people were unable to confide in other villagers as living in such a small, cohesive community came at a price that no one kept secrets and people found themselves the highlight of village gossip. Yet with Larissa, they knew they could confide in her – she didn't mix with the villagers and so all secrets remained safe.

Larissa knew how important the Scots Pine was to her ancestors. They marked the burial ground of chieftains and warriors, and in other parts marked ancient trackways and crossroads. But this pinewood was like her family, it had always been there for her in moments of joy and sadness, where she could inhale the scent of pine needles and feel at calm. Yet there was one tree that piqued her curiosity. It was not as welcoming as the others; it had a dark energy about it. She had tried to hug it a few times to get over any animosity it had towards her, but she was repelled immediately away. It didn't frighten her, but she knew it was not the same as the other trees.

The ground become stickier with the damp earth, she spotted the flooded part of the woods where a natural hollow in the ground created a shallow pond for wildlife, and she knew she was nearly there.

The sound of twigs snapping under her boots was the only sound now, and the tall pine lured her towards the muddy earth around it, where she proceeded to spread her woollen cloak on the damp ground and knelt down before it, almost as if she were worshipping its magnificence. She brought out her tarot cards and shuffled them tenderly. This tree had been calling to her spiritually for some months now, and she would find out what it sought from her.

She looked up at the canopy of pine needles and asked the question: "What is it that you wish me to know," and with that she spread the cards in front of her and lightly ran her finger across them until she felt that familiar tingle in her shoulders. That was the sign for the card that answered her question. She turned the card over tentatively. It was a Major Arcana card, which meant the message was a strong one: it was the Moon card. What could this mean? Normally it represented illusion, deception and something unseen in the shadows. The meaning of it in response to her question was not clear to Larissa, so she drew a clarification card. It was another Major Arcana card: The devil! She went with the item that most stood out to her on the card design, the chains that bound the naked man and woman to the devil. She was chained to something, that much she understood now, but to something that she couldn't see, hence the moon card.

Then something extraordinary happened. Her

vision slowly went out of focus, her eyes saw the two cards merge and she felt rooted to the spot, unable to move. She felt compelled to look up at the canopy of needles and saw a mist descend slowly in swirls around her. The tree grew luminous, almost as if it were bathed in green light. Then the tree spoke to her, not with words, but with thoughts and images, its branches like antenna giving out messages.

She saw the universe being created through good and bad energy crashing together. She saw that the Earth's moon had a good and evil side to it. The two sides fought each other, spinning around violently until the Earth's gravity trapped the moon as its slave. Lucky for the Earth, the good side of the moon-faced planet and protected it from its evil side so that it could not cause chaos on Earth.

And after millennia of observing the galaxy around it as it orbited the earth, the dark side of the moon was visited by humans in a spacecraft. The special suits they wore as they walked on its barren landscape protected them from the dark energy emitted from that side of the moon. But the dark side sensed something organic in the spacecraft: some tree seeds that were going to be used for experiments with moon dust. The dark side of the moon concentrated on the energy it could force the seeds to absorb. Back on Earth, when discovering that the seeds could not be grown in moondust, and that the seeds' structure hadn't changed in space, the seeds were simply sown in compost, just to prove that their trip to the moon hadn't made them infertile. It hadn't. They grew – three very ordinary, earthly trees which grew in small pots on desks, and then as they got bigger, on the floor in the corner by the photocopier. Over time, the saplings were given away to different organisations, and through the passage of time were forgotten about. Larissa understood that she was now under command of the dark side of the moon through this tree, and she was a satellite to its orbit of negative energy.

Larissa didn't remember walking back home and the following morning couldn't even remember visiting that pine tree.

A few days later, as she foraged for herbs and mushrooms in the woods, she chanced upon a stray hiker. He was lost, he explained, he had tried to take a shortcut to the village from the trail he had been walking on, but his navigational skills evidently weren't as good as he thought, and he was desperate for food and shelter. She stared at him blankly for several seconds, and he began to wonder if she maybe didn't speak English. Her black hair gleamed in the sun, her green eyes seemed as luminous as those of a cat; in fact, for some strange reason she reminded him of a black cat about to secure its prey.

Then she spoke in a soft local accent, "Of course. Follow me, I was heading to the village anyway."

And as she took him in the opposite direction to the village, towards the pine tree with the dark energy, he thought he saw the iris of her eyes explode in a riot of autumnal colours, like a supernova.

THE SHOP AT THE END OF THE UNIVERSE

HARRIET HITCHEN

This shop is nothing like the restaurant by the same name. Our visitors don't exchange comic banter while the universe collapses before them. This is my aunt's idea of a witty joke. We're actually a grubby little gift shop on the edge of Dartmoor in holiday season, and a corner shop all the rest of the time selling baked beans and canned beer. We're quite close to a relatively famous inn and the public loos are about 200yrds away. We're open 365 days a year, which feels like eternity – so I suppose for me this is as close as it gets to the vast nothingness of the universe.

When I was a little kid, I remember the day a classmate told us he'd watched a TV documentary. He explained that the earth's spin was slowing down and would eventually stop. We stared agog at the teacher. She confirmed that this was true. I should add that she also explained that this would happen a very long time in the future; but aged 6, even teatime seemed a long time away.

Millenia might mean tomorrow for all I knew.

I remember lying in bed that night forming survival plans. These involved grabbing the nearest shrub as gravity failed and we began drifting into space. I also planned to gather up the black rabbit who lived in the hutch in the garden. My mother and brother would grab hold of the tail of my nightie and we'd all drift safely through space breathing the air put out by our little tree.

Clearly, I learned about the process of photosynthesis long before I learned that space is a vacuum.

My friend at the shop is Ralph. He's like me – a hostage to poverty. He bumps shoulders as he pushes past to get into the storeroom.

"Fridge is out of bottled water. Want to help?"

"Nope."

We're on the late shift. He's eighteen so he's old enough to serve the holidaymakers and derelicts who come in about half an hour before closing for a really nasty bottle of wine. I'm zapping the freezer cabinets with the infrared thermometer. One is on de-icing mode so its figures are way out.

"Do you know what bothers me?"

Ralph shrugs.

"It's taken me this long to realise that when they're talking about setting up colonies on the moon, or sending people to Mars, it won't be people like us. It won't be me."

Ralph grins at me. "What were your science grades again?"

He knows I dropped science at GCSE level. I always dreamed of being a vet, but don't have the brains for it. Mum says it isn't about brains, it's about commitment, but I still dropped science two years ago so that doesn't help me.

"I don't mean the astronauts. I mean when they start sending ordinary folk. You know, when they need cleaners and delivery drivers and space cowboys, and it's a big ark and they're leaving planet earth behind for good."

I suspect Ralph thinks I'm talking about being left behind when he goes off to uni – it's in his face – a carefully schooled blankness. He's on his summer break so by the autumn he'll be off to Southampton or Exeter or wherever it is.

In actual fact, I know where he's going. It's Bristol – but don't let him know I know that.

"I think in a way I'm still forming survival plans. It's the shrub and the pet rabbit all over again. I want to believe there's something I can do."

Now he thinks I'm pining because I can see the years rolling away from me while I'm stuck here staffing a tatty little grocery shop for my aunt. But the shop's fine. It's the idea that when they talk about the timeline for advancing space travel, they talk in terms of decades – that's what bothers me. And when they write a list for the first interglactic spaceliner, I imagine myself on it, but it's me as I am now, not me in 70 years or so. Sometimes boys really don't understand me.

And besides, I don't even really care about any of

that. It's all a smokescreen.

At 11pm I wheel in the signboard while he rolls back the awning. He flicks off the lights while I jangle my aunt's keys in my hand, waiting. The summer air is warm.

He says, "Want a lift home?" Then, after my inevitable negative, adds, "See you tomorrow?"

"Yeah." My farewell is a whisper in the night.

His car is black under the single streetlamp from the nearby pub. In the very distance, I swear I can hear the sound of the sea.

I wave as he pulls away, swimming in headlights. The taillights roll red down the hill when I turn in through the garden gate next door to the shop. His offer of a lift is a joke – and I think I'll miss that more than I'll miss him.

The garden is a short slope that smells faintly of moss and sheep. They get everywhere, even with a stone wall and a gate. I have a favourite perch on the top step. The stone flags are cool beneath my seat.

I lie back. I stare at the misty heavens and while the stars turn above me, I feel every inch of the spin that keeps me grounded. And despite feeling like I ought to rage against everything, I don't mind one bit. I never want to leave.

Crumps Barn Studio